BAD PETS

On the Loose!

ALLAN ZULLO

D1166037

Scholastic Inc.

To Josie and Lucy Rodell, with hopes they won't ever be as naughty as the animals in this book . . . well, maybe just a little bit.
— A.Z.

ISBN 978-0-545-46041-5

12 11 10 9 8 7 6 5 4 3 2 1   12 13 14 15 16 17/0

Printed in the U.S.A.   40
First Scholastic printing, September 2012

CONTENTS

ANIMAL ANTICS

Is there no end to the ridiculous and outlandish things that our pets and other animals sometimes do? Every day there are new cases of animals turning into rogues and ruffians, tricksters and pranksters. There's a reason why the English language has such words as *jailbird*, *monkey business*, and *horseplay*. Whether they walk on two legs or four, or have feathers or scales, mammals, reptiles, and birds are always doing something silly or shocking.

Some of their wackiest antics have been documented in *Bad Pets: True Tales of Misbehaving Animals*, published by Scholastic. But one book can't come close to covering all the naughtiness of the world's animals. So here is another lighthearted collection of true stories of animal mischief ranging from the absurd to the zany.

For example, you'll read about the dog that drove off in a motor home, leaving his master behind . . . the deer that rang a woman's doorbell at all hours of the day and night . . . the squirrels that kept stealing miniature American flags . . . the horse that jumped into a family's swimming pool and refused to get out . . . the bear that barged into a restaurant and ate four pizzas while customers scattered . . . the parrot that drove its owner nuts by mimicking the ringtones on his cell phone . . . the moose that ended up in a couple's bedroom . . . and a cat that set a house on fire!

Whether they howl, growl, or yowl, one thing is certain: Animals of all kinds are — and always will be — wild and amazing!

THIEVES

DOGGONE JOYRIDE

Woodley the dog paid close attention to how his owner, Richard McCormack, drove his huge motor home. So when McCormack left his rig unattended, Woodley hopped into the driver's seat, released the hand brake, put his paws on the wheel, and drove away.

There was no telling how far Woodley would have gone if a shocked pedestrian hadn't chased after the RV and stopped it.

In 2011, McCormack was planning a cross-country trip in Australia in his 20-ton motor home with Woodley, a two-year-old black German koolie, a medium-size herding dog. During previous road trips, Woodley sat in the passenger's seat, carefully watching his master drive.

While in Darwin, Northern Territory, McCormack parked his RV outside a mechanic's shop, where the parking lot sloped toward a busy street. After McCormack stepped out of the rig to talk to the mechanic, Woodley jumped into the driver's seat, released the hand brake on the dashboard, and took the motor home for a spin.

"I came out and saw the bus going down the road," McCormack told NT News. "I couldn't believe it."

Phil Newton was walking by when he did a double take after seeing a dog behind the wheel of a giant motor home rolling down the street. "I thought, 'What the . . . !'" he told NT News. "This was weird, even for the Territory." He said it would not have been such a comical sight had the dog not been sitting in the driver's seat with his paws on the steering wheel.

Once the shock wore off, Newton chased after the RV. He ran fast enough to catch up to the vehicle and then jumped through an open window. Once inside, he pulled on the hand brake and brought an end to Woodley's solo ride.

"It ran for a couple of hundred meters, swerved across the road, went up on the footpath and was just about to run into a parked car when I stopped it," Newton said.

To prevent Woodley from pulling off another theft, McCormack modified the hand brake so the dog couldn't release it. Today, all is forgiven. McCormack declared, "He's still my best mate."

UNBEARABLE CAR THIEVES

As improbable as it seems, bears steal cars.

In one case, a bear broke into a family's auto, trashed the inside, and took it for a short ride before crashing it.

In summer 2011, Brian McCarthy and his family from Pleasanton, California, were asleep in their Lake Tahoe vacation cabin. Suddenly, they were awakened at about 3:30 A.M. by the horn from their Toyota Prius that was parked in the driveway. They also heard strange growling sounds coming from inside the closed-up car.

McCarthy told the *Contra Costa Times*, "We were looking out of our bedroom window and from our view, you could look down and see the bear in the car, and its arms were just flailing all over the place, through the windows and everything."

The frustrated, angry black bear kicked, scratched, bit, and tore at the interior of the car, trying to force his way out. During his rampage, the bear ripped open the seats, bit a chunk out of the steering wheel, and damaged the Prius's gearbox, shifting the car into neutral. "The car was rocking," said McCarthy. He called 911, and when he looked out the window again, the Prius was gone.

From the safety of their cabin, his wife, CeCe, and their son, Dylan, watched helplessly as the Prius with the bear inside slowly rolled down the sloping driveway. As the car picked up speed, it coasted across the street, bounced off a few boulders, hopped a small rock wall, and finally came to rest on the porch steps of a neighbor's house.

After tearing up the inside of the car for about 30 minutes, the bear eventually got out of the Prius and fled into the woods before sheriff's deputies arrived.

"He had ripped out the backseat," CeCe told KNTV News. "There's nothing left inside of our Prius. Gone. He destroyed the driver's side door on the inside."

What was so perplexing was how the bear got into the car in the first place, because the unlocked doors had been closed and no windows were broken. However he got in, the door somehow closed behind him. The family also couldn't understand why the bear had targeted their Prius. "There wasn't any food in there," McCarthy said.

The car was considered a total loss.

Apparently bears like to steal Toyotas because a year earlier, a family in Larkspur, Colorado, had a similar experience with a hairy car thief.

Ben Story, 17, had parked his 2008 Toyota Corolla next to his house and gone to bed. He had forgotten about the peanut-butter-and-jelly sandwich that he left in the car. That was a mistake, especially in bear country where he lived, because bears have the strongest sense of smell in the animal kingdom — two thousand times more sensitive than a human's and seven times that of a bloodhound's.

Shortly after 2 A.M., a black bear wanted that PB and J, so he opened a door of the unlocked car and climbed in. But after eating the sandwich, the bear couldn't get out because the door had slammed shut. Frustrated, he leaned on the horn.

Ben and his family were sleeping so soundly on the other side of the house that they didn't hear the constant honking. But a neighbor did and called Douglas County sheriff's deputies.

By this time, the bear shoved the gear selector into neutral, sending the vehicle rolling down a hill backward for more than one hundred feet before it crashed into a tree. Prior to the impact, the bear unwittingly sent a warning by turning on the flashers and laying on the horn.

The interior of the car was destroyed. "It was a pretty good size," Ben told KDVR News. "If you look at the inside of the car, there's nothing left at all. You could see it moving around. It took up the entire inside of the car. The destruction is amazing. He tore everything up and managed not to miss one little square inch of the car. He got it all."

Ben's father, Ralph Story, told KDVR, "When the cop came up to the car, he thought it was a bunch of kids goofing around. He put a flashlight on it, and he saw this bear turn around, in the driver's seat, and look at him. And when the cop saw that, he said he never ran so fast in his life. The bear was locked in the car and couldn't get out, and the police didn't know what to do at first."

Deputies eventually attached a long rope to a door handle, opened the door, and let the bear escape. The ordeal lasted about two hours.

Damage to the inside of the Toyota was so extensive that the family's insurance agent declared it a total loss.

Before fleeing into the woods, the bear left a rather unpleasant memento of his crime. Said Ben, "He went to the bathroom in there and it's pretty rank."

BIRDBRAINS

A gang of birds found a way to steal quarters out of a coin machine.

Rob Ridings owned the Shop & Wash Carwash, in Fredericksburg, Virginia, a self-service car wash. The business had an automatic machine that collected coins and dollar bills and gave change.

In 1995, Ridings noticed that, based on the number of car washes, the coin machine had come up short. Oddly, he found dozens of quarters scattered on the ground around the car wash. He initially suspected that a thief — and a careless one at that — had broken into a vending machine or the coin machine. But a careful examination showed that the locks hadn't been damaged and everything looked intact.

Ridings became more perplexed when the next day he found a piece of straw sticking out of the machine's coin cup. When he opened the front of the device, he found a couple of dandelions and a cellophane wrapper from a cigarette package stuffed inside.

Suspecting the thief might be an animal, the owner set up a surveillance camera. Pictures of the perpetrators — yes, there was more than one — revealed that a gang of sneaky starlings was robbing him of hundreds of quarters.

Even more surprising, the birds were working as a team. One bird would enter the machine by going up the coin chute and jimmying the coins loose. The other members of the winged robbers would sit on the chute and wait for the coins to fall. Then they would pick up the coins and fly off. One photograph showed a greedy starling with three quarters in its beak.

Experts say that starlings are fascinated by bright, shiny objects and often will collect them for their nests or to attract a mate. Apparently, a starling was drawn to a shiny quarter that had been inadvertently left in the change cup of the coin machine. The bird picked up the coin and made off with it. Other starlings saw what their fellow bird did and imitated the behavior. Before long, the thieving birds figured out how to work as a team to steal the coins from inside the machine itself.

To stop the thievery, Ridings crammed a paper towel up the chute. The next day, he found the birds had pulled it out. So he used black electrical tape to block the chute. That didn't work, either, because within 24 hours, the feathered filchers had pecked their way through the tape. Finally he found success by plugging the chute with a thick cloth rag. When the birds were unable to pull it out, they gave up and didn't try to steal from him again.

WHAT A CROC!

Elvis the crotchety crocodile didn't like lawn mowers, so he stole one right out of the hands of a worker — while the mower was still running.

The huge 16-foot-long, 1,100-pound saltwater croc lives at the Australian Reptile Park in New South Wales, Australia, and has a reputation for being cranky. He doesn't like anyone near him and he doesn't like noise. The 50-year-old reptile made that clear in 2012 when keeper Billy Collett entered Elvis's enclosure and began mowing the grass around the croc's lagoon.

Angry by the disruption, the ill-tempered crocodile charged out of the water and lunged at the mower — never mind that it was still running. He chomped on the front of the machine and engaged in a tug-of-war with Collett. It wasn't much of a contest. Within seconds, Elvis had yanked the machine out of the keeper's hands.

Tim Faulkner, operations manager at the reptile park, heard Collett yell when the crocodile stole his lawn mower. "Elvis got his jaws around the top of the mower and picked it up," Faulkner told the BBC. "Before we knew it, the croc had the mower above his head and then took it underwater with him."

When Elvis dragged the mower into the lagoon, the machine ran for a few seconds before it drowned. He then rested under the water and watched his submerged catch for more than an hour. "Once he got it, he just sat there and guarded it," said Faulkner. "It was his prize, his trophy. If it moved, then he would attack it again."

While the keeper lured Elvis to the other end of the lagoon with kangaroo meat, Faulkner jumped into the water and retrieved the badly chewed-up mower along with two teeth that Elvis had lost during the commission of his crime. "He has extraordinarily large teeth, much bigger than most crocodiles," Faulkner said. "He punched his teeth through the top casing of the mower."

The lawn mower had cut its last blade of grass. It couldn't be fixed.

The manager said that Elvis is "a big territorial male" and one of the largest crocodiles in New South Wales. The reptile has always been a crabby troublemaker. Before he was captured in the wild, he was attacking fishing boats in Darwin harbor.

SQUIRRELING IT AWAY

A squirrel was caught in the act of stealing. But in his defense, he was being patriotic. The items he was swiping were American flags.

For several days during summer 2011, people noticed that miniature flags were disappearing from the Toledo (Ohio) Police Memorial Garden at the Civic Mall, between the municipal and federal courthouses downtown. There were no suspects, no clues left at the scene to help police catch the perpetrator.

But then the cops got a break. While walking into the office one morning, Lieutenant James Brown spotted the squirrelly bandit taking a flag and a single pink plastic flower from the garden. "I just saw him eyeballing it," Brown told the *Toledo Blade*. "He didn't know I was standing there." The officer whipped out his cell phone and snapped a photo of the culprit.

The squirrel pulled the flower, which was attached to a thin metal stake, out of the ground. Then, using his teeth, he began cutting the small flag away from its wooden staff. The officer said it took the squirrel less than 30 seconds to remove the flag without ripping it or knocking over the staff. "He definitely knew what he was doing," Brown said. "This wasn't his first time."

The suspect, whom police described as a red-and-brown bushy-tailed critter, fled with the flag and flower. "He was too fast," Brown said. "I couldn't catch him."

After some sleuthing, police found the squirrel relaxing a short distance away in his hideaway on a tree branch about 30 feet from the ground. He apparently was showing off his patriotism because woven into his tangled nest of branches and leaves were the red, white, and blue fabric of at least two of the missing small flags. The whereabouts of the flower was not known. But, according to the newspaper, police believe the squirrel had planned to use it to spruce up his nest.

No charges were filed by police, who believe the squirrel acted alone in the thefts.

It's possible the squirrel was inspired by a similar patriotic thief who earlier robbed a Michigan cemetery of about a dozen small American flags.

On Memorial Day 2009, volunteers put miniature flags next to gravestones of nearly one thousand veterans buried at the Mount Hope Cemetery in Port Huron. Over the following days, cemetery workers noticed that the flags were disappearing, yet the wooden staffs were still in the ground.

At first, workers couldn't figure out what had happened to the flags. Then cemetery superintendent Ron Ceglarek caught the thief red-handed, or more accurately, red-pawed. It was a squirrel with a fondness for Old Glory.

The squirrel got up on his hind legs, tore a small American flag from a staff next to a gravestone, rolled it up, and carried it to a waiting mate who was building a nest in a nearby tree. "If I didn't see it and I didn't follow the squirrel, I never would have believed it," Ceglarek told the Port Huron *Times Herald*. "It looked like he had a little bandana in his mouth."

Ceglarek soon collected about a dozen staffs with flags missing. "[The squirrel] plucked them right off," he said. "Clean as a whistle."

The nest, which was about 45 feet up a spruce tree, became an attraction for cemetery visitors because it was draped in red, white, and blue. Said Ceglarek, "Why use leaves when you can get flags?"

KING OF THE CAT BURGLARS

Dusty has become one of the world's most famous cat burglars.

For several years, the brown-and-white feline has been prowling the streets of a neighborhood in San Mateo, California, at night, stealing hundreds of items. He gained notoriety in 2011 when special night-vision video cameras caught him bringing home some of his ill-gotten gains. He was so skilled at stealing that the neighbors called him "Klepto the cat," named after the mental disorder kleptomania, which is the irresistible urge to steal trivial items.

His owners, Jean Chu and Jim Coleman, figured the cat had stolen 600 items in the Beresford Park neighborhood during a four-year period beginning in 2007, shortly after the couple adopted him as a kitten from the Peninsula Humane Society. "I noticed a piece of latex glove on the bed one morning and told my husband he should do a better job cleaning up his work stuff," Chu, a dentist, told the *San Francisco Chronicle* in 2011. "He said, 'It wasn't me. I think it was the cat.'"

Soon the cat was bringing home all sorts of goodies, such as gloves, towels, toys, swimsuits, grocery bags, bubble wrap, baseball caps, stuffed animals, shoes, and socks. "It's work," Coleman told the newspaper. "Every time I go out to get the paper in the morning, I have to pick up after him. Sometimes he brings things that are sort of expensive. I get a little worried about that."

Chu started keeping a log of Dusty's haul, which averaged three or four items a week. His record for the most items in one night? A whopping eleven! Chu would wash each stolen item and try to return it to the rightful owner. If she couldn't find the person, she stored the loot in boxes in the dining room.

Dusty especially liked swimsuits. He even swiped a neighbor's bikini bottom that had been left out to dry, and came back ten minutes later for the top.

Most of the neighbors put up with his thievery. "If we're missing something, we know where to go," a neighbor told KGO News.

Chu said that the neighbors don't complain. "I think they find it kind of funny."

When KGO broadcast the story, neighbor Sean Somers saw two of his missing swimsuits on television. He got them back, but there were still other things missing from the Somerses' home. "I am missing a chair, so maybe [it was Dusty]," Sean's mother joked.

Dusty was busted during his late-night rounds in 2011 by night-vision video cameras installed outside his home by the Animal Planet network for its series *Must Love Cats*. The video showed Dusty returning home after several burglaries with clothing, a stuffed toy, and a bra.

Ever since Dusty's exploits were aired on television, the cat burglar has gained instant fame around the world. David Letterman flew Dusty and his human family to New York to appear on his TV show. Chu and Coleman have been interviewed on radio stations from as far away as Sydney, Australia.

Unwilling to keep him locked in at night, Dusty's owners tried to crimp his thieving ways by putting a bell on his collar to warn neighbors that the cat burglar was on the loose. That was good news for neighbor Kelly McLellan, who had her bikini stolen. "You can hear him," she told KGO reporter Vic Lee. "Even inside your house, you'll hear a bell ringing, and you know he's in your backyard — or has just left your backyard with something."

The bell seemed to be working. He hadn't brought anything home for days. But then a few weeks later, Chu found a glove. "It's not one of ours," she told Lee. "I guess he's back at it."

COPY CATS

Unlike Dusty, some cat burglars specialize in stealing one kind of item.

Take Gus, for instance. The two-year-old cat had swiped more than 60 types of footwear from unsuspecting residents in his New Zealand neighborhood, according to the *Daily Telegraph*.

Meredith Kelly, Gus's owner, said that in 2011 the cat focused on filching nothing but shoes from nearby places. After stealing a shoe, he often would return to the scene of the crime for the other one. "At first I thought it was a bit funny, then a bit weird, now it has gone too far," Kelly told the newspaper.

Gus had brought home everything from hiking boots to sandals to children's shoes. He usually announced his ill-gotten trophies with a loud meow. "He either leaves the things in the hallway or, if they're too big to get through the cat flap, on the step," Kelly said.

She has tried to find the shoes' owners by leaving the stolen footwear in a box outside her home, but few have claimed them.

Houdini the cat just couldn't resist stealing garden gloves. Nothing else — just garden gloves.

The black-and-white feline roamed Seattle's Phinney Ridge neighborhood searching for gloves that had been left lying on the ground or on chairs and tables.

He never took pairs, only singles, and brought dozens of them to the front porch of his owner.

At the end of the driveway, Houdini's owner, who asked not to be identified, set out an orange bucket chock-full of pilfered gloves. A note in a clear plastic sleeve attached to the bucket shows a picture of the handsome cat and reads:

> Meet Houdini. You may have seen him around the block. He is very friendly and a very curious cat. Houdini especially likes GLOVES. He searches them out and brings them back to the front porch. We are really sorry for the inconvenience, so we are creating this Glove Lost & Found in hopes the gloves get back to their rightful hands.

"I would come home, and it looked like someone laid out an art collection of single gloves," Diano Garcia, the owner's roommate, told KING News in 2010. "Most people just come by and laugh. They read the sign, and it's funny for them."

Neighbor Ramon Shiloh was a victim of Houdini's. "I've lost latex gloves," he told KING. "I do a lot of artwork. And I've seen my own latex gloves in the driveway. If there were one-handed gardeners out there, they wouldn't care, but I want my glove."

Oscar the cat chose underwear — especially kids' undies — as his favorite thing to steal and bring home. He was so good at his criminal activity that his alarmed owners ratted on him to the police in 2010.

A year earlier, Peter and Birgitt Weismantel, of Southampton, England, adopted the 13-year-old tan-and-white cat from the Cats Protection League. Oscar loved the elderly couple and they loved him back. To show how grateful he was about his new home, he began bringing them gifts — stolen ones. At first they were things such as gardening gloves and socks, but then he zeroed in on underwear — men's, women's, and children's.

His haul of unmentionables continued to grow until he had swiped more than 70 pairs — including a ten-day period when he brought home at least one pair of children's underpants every day. By this time, the Weismantels feared neighbors might think a weird person was on the loose taking their underwear. So the couple felt duty-bound to alert the local police and squeal on their cat.

The cops took down the information, but chose not to arrest Oscar, although he was listed as a feline of interest.

"It's all a bit mysterious," Peter told the BBC. "We don't know where he's getting the items from, because there are no children living near us. He might be going quite far."

Even though they discovered their adopted cat had turned into a notorious thief, the Weismantels refused to punish him or return him to the cat adoption agency. "We feel that he is bringing us presents as a token of appreciation, an offer to help pay his way," said Peter.

His wife, Birgitt, told www.thisishampshire.net, "We fell in love with him before he started taking all these things. It was just so touching to see him come home every day with something for us. We can't give him back now as he makes such an effort with all these gifts."

INSIDE JOB

A cat with a love for gold got himself and his owner in trouble.

A woman in the small Russian town of Kamensk-Uralsky contacted the police in 2011 and told them that her gold jewelry, worth thousands of dollars, had been stolen.

When the cops showed up, they couldn't find any signs of a break-in, so they focused the investigation on the woman's close friends and relatives who might have had access to the house. Suspicion soon turned to some relatives who had spare house keys. Still, the police couldn't crack the case.

Meanwhile, the woman's friends and relatives were annoyed at her for even thinking they would steal her gold jewelry, let alone being forced to undergo intense questioning by the cops.

They had reason to be upset, especially when the real jewel thief "confessed." Yep, it was her cat. A few days after she reported the crime, he pranced in front of her carrying one of her missing gold rings in his mouth. Only then did she realize what he had done. The cat had found where she had originally concealed her jewelry and, one by one, had taken each piece to a new hiding place. She soon recovered her stolen gold earrings, rings, and necklaces.

Embarrassed by her cat's thievery, the woman called the police and told them to end the investigation because she had found the guilty party. That was the easy part. The hard part was phoning her friends and relatives and offering her deepest apologies.

A goat-riding monkey was sneaking onto a farmer's land in China and stealing his vegetables.

Ye Shu, of Donguan, Guangdong Province, told authorities in 2011 that shortly after an acrobatic circus arrived in the area, some of his vegetables were being picked without his permission. Deciding to investigate, the farmer kept watch over his field. To his shock, he saw a monkey on the back of a large, long-haired, horned goat show up at his field. The two animals then plucked veggies out of the ground and ate them, Ye claimed.

"This has been going on for two weeks since the acrobatic troupe was first stationed here," he told a reporter. Ye said the clever monkey would stand on the goat's back to make sure the coast was clear before launching his raids. "If the monkey sees that nobody is working in the field, he rides in on the goat, and they start eating and causing trouble," Ye claimed.

A circus spokesman admitted no one had been watching over the animals after they had finished their part of the performance. As a result, the two were free to engage in their criminal activities. "We have compensated Ye Shu, and we are sorry for our neglect," said Wu Jun, the troupe's leader. Wu said he had hired more animal keepers to prevent the pair from getting into further mischief.

FEATHERED FELON

In New Zealand, a wild parrot from a species known for mischief swiped the passport of a Scottish tourist and disappeared with it into a forest.

The Scotsman, who asked to remain anonymous, was on a tour bus in the rugged Fiordland region in 2009. The area is the home of thousands of native keas, highly intelligent green parrots with powerful curved beaks and long, sharp claws. The birds are known as the "clowns of the mountains," because they have a tendency to make people laugh at their antics. But they also have a tendency to make people angry. Keas have been caught vandalizing parked cars by stripping the rubber off of windshield wipers, breaking off side-view mirrors, and even puncturing tires.

And they like to steal things, as the hapless Scottish visitor learned. During a rest stop in the wilderness, the bus driver opened the luggage compartment. From a nearby tree, a crafty kea was watching him and admiring a brightly colored travel pouch in the open compartment. The pouch contained, among other things, the Scotsman's passport.

With the driver's back to the parrot, the kea swooped down and grabbed the pouch. When the driver turned around and saw the bird with the pouch in its beak, he yelled at it. Startled by the driver's shouts, the kea flew off into the thick forest with the pouch and was never seen again.

British officials told him it would take up to six weeks before he received a replacement passport and cost him $400 in addition to all the extra expenses of staying in New Zealand.

"Being Scottish, I've got a sense of humor, so I did take it with humor," he told the *Southland Times*. "But obviously there is a side of me that is still raging."

RASCALS

HAVING A BALL

A police dog was patrolling on the sidelines during a soccer match to keep fans from bothering the players. But he became his own worst enemy when he stole the ball — during the game!

A German shepherd named Agil was working with his police handler at a match between Boa and UEC in Brazil in 2011. Because Agil was normally quite obedient, his handler had taken him off the leash.

The dog was resting on the ground, watching the action, when suddenly he decided to enter the game. As a UEC player was attempting a pass, Agil charged from the sidelines onto the field and snatched the ball away from him. The dog then began playing with the ball as if he owned it.

With his butt in the air and his tail wagging, he moved the ball around the field while the crowd cheered and laughed. However, neither the players nor his handler found his antics funny. After Agil gnawed on the ball for a bit, his embarrassed handler walked out onto the field. The dog tried to dodge him, but then realized his brief playtime was over. The handler put him back on his leash and led him off the field to a standing ovation from the fans. Taken to the back of the sidelines, the dog was given a stern reprimand, judging by the way his tail ended up tucked between his legs.

UEC lost the match 3–2, prompting a soccer blogger to write that the team should sign Agil "for his ability to disarm an attack and maul any opponent dumb enough to challenge him for the ball."

THUMBED OUT

The mascot for a minor-league baseball team became the first dog officially thrown out of a professional baseball game by an umpire — for pooping on the field.

A one-year-old black Labrador retriever named Master Yogi Berra had been trained to perform between innings of home games of the Greensboro (North Carolina) Grasshoppers, a minor-league team affiliated with the Miami Marlins. One of his tricks was to fetch a ball shot from a special handheld cannon.

Before the top of the fourth inning of an early season game in 2009, Master Yogi Berra (who was named after the New York Yankees' Hall of Fame catcher) dashed from first base out to deep center field to track down the shot ball. While still on the run, he scooped up the ball in his mouth, turned, and scampered toward home plate. But on his return, he stopped behind second base, squatted, and left a nasty memento on the grass. The crowd roared with laughter. Then he ran in a big circle before reaching home.

Although the fans thought it was hilarious, home plate umpire Jason Hutchings didn't. In fact, he was so peeved that he threw the dog out of the game in what is believed to be the first canine ejection in pro-baseball history.

Some fans thought the dog was making a statement about his team, because the Grasshoppers eventually lost the game to the Asheville Tourists 9-6.

But Grasshoppers general manager Donald Moore claimed that the dog was suffering from a stomach virus. "When you gotta go, you gotta go," Moore told reporters after the game. "I don't know the rulebook like the back of my hand, but apparently a dog can't do his business on the field. Let's hope this is an isolated incident, and Yogi can learn from this experience."

APPLE PIE–EYED

A wild elk got so drunk she ended up stuck in a tree. That's right, *in* a tree.

The sloshed elk made headlines in Saro, Sweden, in 2011 after she became intoxicated. No, she hadn't raided a tavern or a liquor store. She got smashed by eating rotting apples that had fallen on the ground and were fermenting in a natural process that produced alcohol.

Stumbling around a neighborhood at night, she devoured enough rotting apples to get drunk. Still, she wanted more. After she came across an apple tree in a backyard, she stood on her hind legs to reach some of the forbidden fruit still dangling on the branches when she lost her balance and became snagged in the fork of the tree.

"I returned home from work and discovered an elk stuck in an apple tree with only one leg left on the ground," neighbor Per Johansson told the local newspaper. "I thought it looked pretty bad, so I called the police who sent out an on-call hunter. But while we were waiting, the neighbors and I started to saw down some of the branches, and then the hunter arrived with a saw as well."

Johansson said the group tried but failed to free the elk, so they called firefighters, who used ropes to help her slide out of the branches and crash to the ground. Instead of getting up and staggering off, she passed out in the yard. They decided to leave her there to sleep it off. The next morning, she slowly got to her feet and, nursing a mean hangover, wobbled away.

"My neighbor recognized it as the animal that almost ran into her car the day before," said Johansson. "She was pretty sure the elk was already under the influence."

Three days later, Swedish authorities received a report of another drunken elk — but this one turned out to be a thief as well. The beast had stumbled off with a family's backyard swing set!

It happened in the town of Storebro, about 180 miles from Saro. Once again, an elk became drunk from eating fermented apples. Somehow in his drunken stupor, his antlers got snagged on the swing set. Unable to get rid of the playground equipment, he took it with him.

According to the Swedish news agency TT, the homeowner told police he arrived home Wednesday to discover bits of apple littering his yard and his children's swing set was missing. Suspecting a drunken elk, police called a local hunter to track the animal. The four-legged thief got away, but the swing set was found propped against a tree in the woods.

THRILL RIDE

A black bear hitched a ride in the back of an open garbage truck through downtown Vancouver, British Columbia, startling pedestrians along the way.

"The bear was sitting on top of the truck like he was king of the world," conservation officer Alex Desjardins told Canada's *The Globe and Mail*.

The two-year-old male had jumped into a Dumpster in North Vancouver and was foraging for food one day in 2011. He was so intent on scarfing down all he could that he failed to act quickly enough when a garbage truck picked up the bin and dumped the contents in the back. The driver was unaware that along with the trash went the bear.

The Dumpster-diving bruin then became a hitchhiking bear. He stood up in the back as the garbage truck drove for miles through the bustling city and into the heart of downtown. When the truck stopped near the main post office, people saw the bear and called authorities.

"Initially I had a hard time believing it," Desjardins told the Vancouver newspaper *The Province*. "The dispatcher said, 'It's not April Fools'.'"

By the time Desjardins arrived, a crowd had gathered. Police had cordoned off the area and surrounded the bear, who was still crawling around in the back of the truck. The conservation officer climbed onto the hood of the truck and, using a jab pole with a needle attached to the end, tranquilized the creature. It took about five minutes for the drugs to kick in.

As soon as he dozed off, the bear was placed in a steel container and taken for an overnight stay at an animal facility for examination. Because he was in good health and wasn't aggressive, officials decided to relocate him away from a populated area. They released him in the Squamish Valley with hopes that his hitchhiking days were over.

SQUIRRELLY PRANKSTER

When a false fire alarm went off at an elementary school, officials assumed a student had pulled it. They questioned the kids but weren't any closer to solving the mystery. Not until officials looked at video from security cameras did they unmask the culprit — a wily squirrel.

In 2010, students were evacuated after an alarm was activated inside a kitchen storeroom of Blackburn Elementary School in Ellenton, Florida. Firefighters searched the school but found no fire. Baffled officials questioned kitchen staff, who said no one was in the area when the alarm was pulled.

Maintenance staff reviewed security camera video and discovered a squirrel that had taken up residence in the school kitchen was responsible for the false alarm. The video showed the rascally rodent climbing five feet of plastic conduit that covered the wires of the alarm pull station. After looking around to make sure no one saw him, the squirrel grabbed the lever and set off the alarm. Then it fled.

"We've had kids pull fire pull stations, but we've never had an animal do it," Todd Henson, director of maintenance and operations, told the Sarasota *Herald-Tribune*.

The video was shown to North River Fire Department officials to convince them the false alarm was not the Manatee County School District's fault. If it had been the school's fault, the district would have been fined.

The furry prankster was eventually trapped by a pest control unit. Said Henson, "It's really hard to fine a squirrel, so he got a stern lecture and was released outside."

DING DONG . . . WHO'S THERE?

When it comes to pranksters in the animal world, you absolutely, positively have to include the deer that kept punking a Canadian woman. At all hours of the day and night, they would ring her doorbell and run off.

Rose Allin, of Kenora, Ontario, was the victim of deer that seemed to have fun at her expense. In 2010, they scrounged around her yard, eating her flowers. Hoping to keep the invaders out, Allin erected a special fence, but the deer either jumped over it or through it. Next, she doused her remaining plants with a special deer-preventing spray, but the rascals simply ignored it.

It was one thing for the deer to devour her flowers. But it was quite another for them to come up to the front step and ring her doorbell. They did it in the mornings, afternoons, and evenings, sometimes scattering and sometimes staying to watch her reaction. "I just wish they'd stop," she told the *Calgary Sun*.

One time, they rang the doorbell before daybreak. Allin was so angry that when she opened the door, she waved her cane and cursed at them. However, unlike the others, one doe refused to run. Instead, she snorted and scratched the ground in an attempt to scare Allin. It worked. The woman slammed the door.

According to the *Sun*, her nephew warned her not to challenge the deer, telling her, "Auntie, don't do that. Don't you know they could put a hoof right through you?" Or a set of antlers.

Allin covered the doorbell, which made it harder for the deer to press it. Nevertheless, some still managed to ring it.

Assuming the deer weren't ringing her doorbell just for kicks, experts have come up with a possible explanation: A deer used the doorbell as a place to mark its territory by rubbing its scent with its forehead. One or more other deer likewise rubbed their own scent in a sort of turf war. If true, then it was Rose Allin's bad luck that the deer's marking spot happened to be her doorbell.

PARTY ANIMAL

A pit bull looking for a good time broke into a house and partied with two little dogs for nearly an hour, whooping it up and trashing the place until the humans showed up and stopped his fun.

Residents in a Houston, Texas, neighborhood had reported seeing a male pit bull roaming from house to house as if he was searching for someone or something. He didn't appear aggressive or dangerous; and, as it turned out, he wasn't. He just wanted to par-tay.

He finally found his fun house — the residence of Rosie Sanchez, who was at work while her two pets, a Chihuahua and a Yorkshire terrier, were home alone. Neighbor Diana Session noticed the pit bull was outside pawing at the front window of Sanchez's house while the two little dogs were pawing on the window from the inside.

Evidently, they were inviting him to join them, because he went around the back and shoved his way through a poorly locked door. After introductions were made, the fun began and the three of them tore around the house — with an emphasis on *tore*.

During the revelry, Session looked at Sanchez's house and was shocked to see the pit bull was still at the front window but now on the inside with his two new buds — and they were all smiling.

"I'm like, 'Oh my God.' I couldn't believe that dog was in there," Session told KHOU News. Session called animal control and then took pictures through the front window of the frolicking dogs. The pit bull and the Chihuahua — her name was Princess — had quickly become pals.

Alas, the fun ended when the animal-control officer came into the house and collared the pit bull. The dog was taken to Houston's Bureau of Animal Regulation and Care, which planned to find his owner or a new home.

Judging from the condition of the inside, it was one heck of a party. "It was just a mess," recalled Sanchez. The rooms looked like they had been ransacked. Dog food and junk-food wrappers were scattered throughout the house. So were pillows, papers, and DVDs. A pair of candlesticks was broken. Furniture, along with stereo and gaming equipment, was overturned and the couch was damaged. A puddle of urine was underneath her dining room table.

"I mean, you can just see that the dog just tore through so much," Sanchez told the TV station. "It's very amazing to me that he got in."

Her Yorkie and Chihuahua were fine, but seemed a little sad that the party dog had been taken away from them.

CANINE HIJACKER

A dog commandeered a city bus, forced all 25 passengers and the driver off the vehicle, and then held police at bay for 30 minutes.

It was a spur-of-the-moment canine crime perpetrated by a German shepherd named Duke. He was walking down a Miami street in 1973 when a summer storm kicked up. Not wanting to remain outside during the heavy downpour, the dog sought shelter at a covered bus stop where several people were waiting.

When bus No. 139 stopped, the driver opened the door. Duke hopped on board first, causing the would-be passengers to back away, saying they would wait for the next bus. The driver, A. I. Rivera, was so startled that he stood up. Apparently Duke took that to mean the driver's seat was available, so the dog took it.

"The driver reached out to pet the dog," reported Miami Transit Authority superintendent F. M. Fieber. "With his teeth, the dog grabbed hold of his hand but did not break the skin. The driver then removed his hand, himself, and the twenty-five passengers, leaving the bus to the dog."

Duke didn't growl or bark. He just sat in the driver's

seat and looked out the window, waiting for the rain to stop.

Not sure what to do, Rivera flagged down a passing bus. Perplexed, the other driver asked, "What happened? What happened?"

"A dog just took over my bus!" Rivera replied.

Someone ran to the nearest home (this was before cell phones) and called the police. Within minutes, three squad cars arrived. "The police took one look at the dog and stopped in their tracks," a witness told reporters.

Duke wasn't ready to give up his seat. For a while, no one wanted to do anything because they were afraid of him. Finally, a cop got close enough to read the tags on the dog's collar. Learning that his owners, Rolando Rodriguez and his wife, lived nearby, the police brought them to the standoff. The couple then ordered Duke to step off the bus.

The vehicle was back in service 30 minutes behind schedule, but it was empty. The passengers had already been transferred to another bus.

As for Duke, police didn't arrest him. "Duke is a wonderful dog, very gentle," said Mrs. Rodriguez. "But he is very frightened of storms." She said he meant no harm.

Passenger Harold Lee wasn't so sure, telling a reporter, "This was a clear case of a dog-jacking."

PHONE TONE GROAN

Billy the parrot drove his owner crazy because of the bird's amazing talent to imitate the ringtones of a cell phone.

Owner Stuart McNae was forced to change the ringtone on his cell phone five times because of his parrot's antics. For weeks in 2007, McNae, of Huddersfield, West Yorkshire, England, was tricked by his playful blue-fronted Amazon.

Whenever McNae left his cell phone behind in the same room where Billy was perched, the winged trickster would mimic the sound of an incoming call, causing the 54-year-old man to dash back to answer the phone, only to find out there was no one on the line. Then Billy would burst into giggles.

"He waits for me to leave the room before he does it," he told the *Sun*. "I'll rush downstairs to find it's Billy."

The bus-firm worker changed the ringtone from the Nokia theme to Lou Bega's "Mambo Number 5," the BBC Match of the Day tune, Booker T and the MGs' "Soul Limbo," and Bob Marley's "No Woman, No Cry." Each time, the talented parrot learned the new ringtone. "I now have the theme from *A Fistful of Dollars*,"

McNae said at the time. "It won't be long before he's got that, too."

RUDE AWAKENING

A blackbird tormented a British family for months, waking everyone up at the crack of dawn by mimicking the siren from an ambulance.

Nathan and Alison Talbot and their two children were roused from their beds at 5 A.M. every morning by the annoying bird. "It's only a tiny bird, but the sound is so incredibly loud, there is no drowning it out," Alison told the *Daily Mail* at the time. "It is so realistic, the first time I heard it I thought it was a real ambulance."

For more than four months in 2008, the Talbots, from North Somerset, England, had to put up with the unwanted wake-up call. Alison said the family was getting exhausted from the bird's early-morning siren imitations.

Nathan said he tried to shoo the bird away, but it always returned to their yard. "When I first heard the sound, it was funny," he said. "But now it's just annoying. It keeps us and all our neighbors awake."

As if that wasn't irritating enough, the bird also confused the Talbots by imitating a cell phone ringtone and a car alarm. The bird wasn't deliberately targeting the Talbots but rather was making the sounds it heard every day to attract a mate, said bird expert Steven Dudley, of the British Ornithologists' Union. "In twenty years I've only seen one other blackbird which could do this, so it is very unusual."

Apparently, the bird's efforts to woo a mate were taking much longer than the Talbots had hoped. From April through July, it kept adding new sounds to its range of imitations. "The bird is obviously very good at mimicking," Alison said. "My husband tried wolf-whistling at it the other day, and it wolf-whistled right back at him."

"DON'T LEAVE ME!"

Security guards rushed through a city train in a frantic search for a woman crying for help. They soon discovered that the female in distress wasn't a human, but a parrot.

During the Christmas holiday rush in 1900 in Chicago, a crowded elevated train (known as "the L") left the Halsted Street station when all of a sudden passengers heard a woman's voice plead, "Don't leave me! Don't leave me! For heaven's sake, don't leave me in this place!"

Security guards pushed passengers aside as they worked their way through the packed car in a desperate effort to locate the troubled woman. But they couldn't find her. As the L neared the next station, the guards questioned some of the passengers and concluded that the woman — one with an extremely loud voice — had been left behind at the Halsted Street station.

"But their conclusions were set aside quickly when the train slowed up at the Marshfield Avenue station," according to the *Chicago Chronicle*. "Again the owner of the voice, in a low weird tone, cried between what sounded like sobs: 'For heaven's sake, take me out of this place or I'll die!' Again the guards and passengers, in a fit of astonishment, renewed their search for the speaker, thinking that she was in great danger of her life."

One guard looked under each seat of the train until he found the source of the cries for help. Instead of a human, he found a green parrot in a cage that was wrapped in a heavy brown paper. The bird had pecked a hole through the paper and was pleading to get out — or at least off the L. "When discovered, it was a pitiful-looking sight," the newspaper reported. "With its bill wide open, its green feathers disheveled, and its head protruding through the cage, the parrot remained" upset.

Because no one on the L claimed ownership of the bird, a guard stayed with it until the train reached the end of the line. Then the parrot was turned over to the lost-and-found department.

Several hours later, an embarrassed woman showed up and claimed ownership of it. She told employees that she had brought the parrot with her on the L. The woman was so focused on her holiday plans that she had forgotten about the parrot when she got off at the Halsted Street station. Not until she was nearly home did she realize she had left the bird behind.

NO BUTTS ABOUT SHIRLEY

An orangutan nicknamed Smoking Shirley had a bad habit — cigarettes.

While living in a zoo in Malaysia, the 20-year-old adult ape picked up lit cigarettes that had been tossed into her pitlike enclosure by thoughtless visitors. Observing how humans smoked, she began smoking and became hooked.

Many unthinking people found it hilarious to see an orangutan puffing away on cigarettes. But when Malaysian wildlife officials found out about her habit, they weren't amused. In 2011, they seized Smoking Shirley from the state-run zoo where she had been living for years. They took her to the Melaka Zoo in a neighboring state and made it clear that she would never smoke again.

Melaka Zoo director Ahmad Azhar Mohammed said Smoking Shirley wasn't provided any more cigarettes, because they are as bad for apes as they are for humans. "Smoking is not normal behavior for orangutans," he told the Associated Press (AP). "She had formed a habit after mimicking human beings who were smoking around her, but fortunately, she wasn't addicted."

The orangutan was forced to quit "cold turkey" — in other words, all at once. After appearing moody for a day or two in her new surroundings, she accepted the ban on cigarettes. She developed a regular appetite for food and showed no signs of depression or illness. Results from blood tests and a physical exam indicated that she wouldn't suffer any adverse health effects.

Orangutans, which are native to rain forests in Borneo and the Indonesian island of Sumatra, can live up to about 60 years in captivity. Having kicked the habit, she was sent to a Malaysian wildlife center in Borneo, where she was once again known only as Shirley.

OUT ON A LIMB

Midnight the cat went out on a limb, causing a chain reaction of troubles for her owner.

In 1986, the feline sneaked out of the rural home of Ronald Brodie, of Cape Coral, Florida, and climbed a pine tree, where she took a little snooze. But when it was time to come down, Midnight got scared and remained frozen on a branch about 40 feet from the ground.

Brodie tried to sweet-talk her down and entice her with cat food, but she still wouldn't move. Getting more annoyed by the minute, Brodie started climbing the tree to rescue her. When he was about 20 feet up, a branch snapped and Brodie plunged to the ground. "I landed on my butt and left leg," he told reporters later. "The shock of the fall made it hard for me to move."

He called for help, but no one heard him. In desperation, he came up with a questionable solution. "The only thing I could think of was to set the grass on fire in the field," Brodie recalled. He thought that would attract someone.

Flames made his other cat, Jingles, meow loudly from inside the house, waking up Brodie's fiancée, who called the fire department. When firefighters arrived, they extinguished the small blaze and treated Brodie for back and leg injuries. Watching it all from above was Midnight, still in no mood to leave her perch.

Only after firefighters had left and Brodie had been put to bed to recover did Midnight get down on her own as if nothing had happened.

Brodie said he would never go out on a limb for a cat again, declaring, "Next time she can stay up in the tree."

INTRUDERS

PIZZA LOVER

A black bear boldly strolled into a Canadian pizza parlor at dinnertime and, as startled guests and workers moved away, helped himself to . . . what else? . . . pizza.

The bear with a taste for Italian cuisine showed up in 2011 outside Fat Tony's, a popular restaurant in the ski village of Whistler, British Columbia. Through an open back door, two female employees saw him pawing at a garbage can a few feet away. Then the bear walked in, causing people inside to back away from the stainless-steel counter that separated the kitchen from the main dining area.

"The bear stood up over the counter and grabbed a pizza off the display and started eating it," employee Colin Mont told the *Vancouver Sun*. "The girls stood back and let him do what he needed to do."

After polishing off slices of the restaurant's famous beef-and-blue-cheese pizza, the 400-pound bear selected slices from another freshly baked pie and devoured that one, too. He then sampled two others fresh out of the oven, including a vegetarian and one with cheeseburger toppings.

Meanwhile, workers and customers took pictures and shot video of the pizza-loving bear. Video posted to YouTube showed the bear licking his lips while eating the pizza. People in the crowd were laughing after one person cracked, "You better give a good tip, bud."

Onlooker Nicole Smith told a reporter, "He was having difficulty not slipping off the stainless-steel counter, but was able to reach up and grab all the pizza slices he wanted. He was eating slice by slice and had impeccable manners — for a bear."

After he had gobbled up all the pizza that had been sitting out, conservation officials who had arrived on the scene ordered customers to leave the restaurant. Then employees banged on pots and pans to drive the bear out of the place. Nothing in the pizza parlor was damaged other than the garbage can, which was destroyed.

That was probably the last time the bear would ever get to gorge himself on pizza. Days later, the very same bear was caught by conservation officials and relocated to a wilderness area far from any pizza joint.

SEE YA LATER, ALLIGATOR!

A six-foot-long alligator that had been watching two house cats playing in a screened-in patio thought they would make a tasty snack. So while their owner was at work, he broke into the house and pursued the cats from room to room.

Fortunately, his attempted double murder was thwarted — but not before he scared the homeowner out of her wits when she came home and found him hissing at her in the bathroom.

Alexis Dunbar, of Palmetto, Florida, lived near a pond that was frequented by gators. She noticed one such reptile had been casing her place for a couple of weeks, eyeballing her two frisky cats, Jayde and Dymond, as they hopped in and out of the cat door that led to and from an enclosed patio. Dunbar assumed the cats were

55

perfectly safe because her backyard had a chain-link fence to keep predators out.

But this alligator was determined to eat those cats. So late one night in 2011 while Dunbar was at work, he made his move. Somehow he sneaked under the fence, went across the yard, busted through the patio screen, and squeezed through the cat door. At some point in the break-in, he cut himself.

Sensing danger, the freaked-out cats bounded from one room to another. All the while, for hours and hours, the gator methodically stalked them throughout the house — the kitchen, the living room, down the hall to Dunbar's bedroom and bathroom, and then into the guest bathroom.

When Dunbar returned home from work around noon, she received the shock of her life. There, in the guest bathroom, just a few feet away, was the mean-looking alligator with his mouth open, hissing at her and poised to attack. "I didn't know what to do," Dunbar told WFLA News. "It was unreal. I felt invaded."

Dunbar screamed for her boyfriend, who propped a small table on its side to keep the gator in the bathroom.

Seeing a trail of blood throughout the house, Dunbar at first feared that one or both of her cats had been eaten by the gator. "My cats are like my daughters," she said. Thankfully, she found them shaken but unharmed.

Dunbar recognized the intruder as the one that had been staking out the cats for two weeks. "He must have looked at them as food every day," she said. "He finally got bold and came up on the bank. My neighbor said she heard my porch things being knocked over at 3 A.M. So he must have been here all night until I got home at noon. My furniture was all moved around." She said her blinds were all crooked, too.

An officer from the Florida Fish and Wildlife Conservation Commission arrived with a trapper who lassoed the gator, dragged him out of the house, and took him away for good. After that, Dunbar kept the cat door closed permanently so her pets couldn't get out — and so another gator couldn't get in.

A SMASHING ENTRANCE

A deer with an apparent love for tacos and enchiladas didn't bother walking through the door of a Mexican restaurant. Instead, he crashed through the eatery's front window, scattering startled diners and workers alike.

The 200-pound buck made his smashing entrance on a Sunday afternoon in 2011 while patrons were eating late lunches and watching football on TV at Taco Mac restaurant in Alpharetta, Georgia. Shards of window glass flew in all directions.

"The deer comes straight through the parking lot, smashes through the window right in front of the host stand," restaurant manager Adam Buckner told the *Atlanta Journal–Constitution*.

Video from Taco Mac's surveillance camera showed the deer running around and skidding between tables, as if he had swallowed too much hot sauce and was in a mad dash for water. In truth, he never slowed down to sample any of the Mexican fare.

He finally made his way toward the rear of the restaurant, where a worker opened the door and let him out onto the back patio. But the buck didn't stop there. The aroma of refried beans and chimichangas possibly was too enticing for him, because now he wanted back into the restaurant. He began head-butting the door, which customers and staff quickly secured.

The deer finally gave up. After jumping off the patio, he leaped over a fence and disappeared. Fortunately, there were no casualties. One customer was nicked in the leg by flying glass, and the deer lost only an antler.

*   *   *

Just days earlier, another buck walked into a New Jersey shoe store and admired himself in the mirror, but obviously didn't find anything that fit him.

Shortly after the Monmouth Mall in Eatontown opened for business, the deer literally went through a side entrance without opening the glass door. Then he ran down the mall concourse and entered Journeys shoe and clothing store. Showing his displeasure over the selection of shoes on sale, he knocked over several displays.

The antlered deer paused in front of a mirror and checked himself out. Whether or not he was pleased with what he saw, he made a couple of charges at the mirror. Then he ran toward store manager Tom Bisogne, who jumped over the counter to avoid getting rammed. Unable to find what he wanted up front, the deer went to the stockroom in the back. That gave employees the opportunity to barricade the stockroom door, trapping the intruder.

New Jersey Division of Fish and Wildlife officers arrived and used a tranquilizer gun to subdue the deer. After he was removed from the store, the buck was examined and found to be in good health. He was then released in a nearby preserve, where he was safe but shoeless.

A young moose dropped in at the home of a surprised couple, ending up in their basement bedroom.

The uninvited guest appeared unexpectedly on a wintry afternoon in 2009 in Spokane, Washington. The calf had been seen earlier tagging along with a sibling and their mama in the couple's wooded neighborhood.

Tony Mantese, owner of the house, told KING News that he saw the moose playing a game of chase with a dog in the snow. "He was running all through the neighborhood, and I saw him going through my backyard and then I heard a crash," Mantese recalled. The calf had come so close to the house that he fell into a large basement window well. As he struggled to get out and rejoin his mother and sibling, he kicked through the basement window and tumbled into the house. He landed in a newly decorated bedroom.

Woody Myers, a Washington Department of Fish and Wildlife biologist trained to tranquilize big-game animals, told the Spokane *Spokesman-Review*, "I got the call around 6 P.M. that there was a moose in somebody's basement. I said, 'You're kidding,' and the officer quite sternly said, 'No I'm not.'"

Because the calf didn't try to bust out of the

bedroom, it was relatively easy for Myers to shoot the animal with a tranquilizer dart. The moose flinched when the dart was shot into his rump, and then he walked around the room for a few minutes before lying down. Myers said. "It went very smoothly."

The bigger problem was getting the moose out of the house. "Five of us used a tarp to take the calf up a narrow stairway," Myers told the newspaper. "It weighed about three hundred and seventy-five pounds, but there wasn't really room there for a three-hundred-and-seventy-five-pound moose and four men, so we just had to heave-and-ho a foot at a time. Then we had to take it through the kitchen and load it into a pickup."

The calf was driven to a wildlife rehabilitation center and kept overnight. Meanwhile, officers tracked down and tranquilized the free-roaming mother and sibling and reunited them with the calf. The trio was then trucked to a remote spot near Mount Spokane and safely released.

THAT'S SOME HORSEPLAY

Caper the retired racehorse wanted to join three teenage boys who were swimming in their screened-in pool. So he did. But once he jumped in, he refused to leave and had to be dragged out hours later with the help of a tow truck.

Alex O'Brien, who was one of the teens, and his family lived in an area of horse pastures and stables in Melbourne, Florida. On a hot summer day in 2011, they were visited by the seven-foot-tall, 1,500-pound stallion who was being boarded on four acres next to the O'Briens' home.

"We were swimming, and the screen door was cracked open," Alex told WOFL News. "He kind of nudged it with his nose and came in [to the pool deck]. I hopped out of the water, grabbed him, and tried walking him out, but he didn't want to go out. So he started backing up."

Looking to cool off, Caper backed up on the five-foot-wide deck until he plopped into the pool. The boys tried for more than two hours to coax the horse up the pool steps, but the six-year-old brown stallion refused. The teens then summoned a veterinarian for help. After making sure the horse wasn't injured, the vet tried to persuade Caper to leave. The stallion wouldn't budge.

The frustrated group then called 911 for assistance from the Brevard County fire department and Brevard County Animal Services and Enforcement. When firefighters arrived, they found the horse calmly standing in chest-deep (for him) water. With the approval of the homeowner, firefighters removed a portion of the screened pool enclosure and called in a heavy-duty wrecker that was normally used to tow fire engines. After the vet sedated Caper, they placed a makeshift sling under him and rigged the harness to the back of the tow truck. Then they hoisted the horse out of the water.

After more than five hours, Caper was back in the pasture. There was no more horsing around for him.

SEAL OF APPROVAL

A baby seal got so lost that he wound up wriggling through a cat door of a New Zealand home and taking a snooze on the couch.

Wildlife officials had been looking for the wayward pup after receiving reports that a small seal had been seen on land in the Tauranga suburb of Welcome Bay in 2011. The pup had made his way from the waterfront, through a residential area, across a busy road, and up the long driveway of Annette Swoffer's home. Then he went under her gate, through her cat door, and up the stairs to her kitchen.

"I was in my office and I heard an awful racket down below," Swoffer told the *Bay of Plenty Times*. "I thought the cats had brought a rabbit or something in, so I went down and had a look — and there's a seal in my kitchen. I'm definitely seeing flippers and not paws. I thought, 'I'm hallucinating, this is just wrong.'"

To make sure she wasn't imagining things, Swoffer summoned a neighbor to verify that, yes, there was a baby seal in her kitchen hanging out with her cats and dog.

Making himself right at home, the young pup eased past Swoffer and her animals and hopped up on her couch and snuggled in for the night. "Then it looked at me with those huge brown eyes," she told the newspaper. "It was so cute and really friendly. I was standing there thinking, 'This is really strange.'"

Swoffer called the Society for the Prevention of Cruelty to Animals. "They were giggling away and I said, 'I'm not drunk, I'm not lying. There's a seal in my house.'"

The SPCA called the Department of Conservation, which had been looking for the lost seal. Chris Clark, biodiversity program manager for DOC, arrived at Swoffer's house and saw it was the same young pup that he had captured earlier in the day in the garden of an elderly couple and had released back into the water.

At Swoffer's house, Clark got the seal into a box and put him in the backseat of the DOC vehicle. But the pup wasn't done causing mischief. As he was being driven away, he got out of his box, climbed into the front seat, and somehow turned on the radio.

The day after the pup was released, Clark received a call about a baby seal wandering around a Welcome Bay neighborhood, no doubt looking for Annette Swoffer's house.

STICKY PAWS

A black bear with a sweet tooth picked the perfect shop to break into — a candy store. He spent his time gorging on hundreds of dollars worth of sugary treats.

Around 6:30 A.M. one morning in 2011, two workers at Ole Smoky Candy Kitchen in Gatlinburg, Tennessee, entered the store through the back door and discovered signs of an intruder. "We turned the light on and saw candy on the floor," Gwatha Kear told the *Mountain Press*. "We could tell something had been here, but we didn't know what. Never in a million years did I think a bear would break in."

But the evidence was all there. The cement floor was covered in paw prints still wet after the bear broke in during a rain shower. Candy, wrappers, and packaging were scattered throughout the back storeroom. Smashed

65

rock candy and nuts were strewn all over the floor. Expensive pecan logs had been chewed on and chunks had been taken out of caramel apples. A whole container of white chocolate–covered pretzels had been consumed.

When Kear and coworker Dorothy Robbins walked to the front of the shop, they saw how the bear got inside — he had busted a hole in the glass front door. The animal had also pooped next to the shop's glass display cases.

"We knew a bear was in there," Robbins told the newspaper. "We could smell it. It left its calling card. We turned the [overhead range] hood on [hoping] we scared it." The workers chose not to search for the bear. "If I had seen it, I would have died in my tracks."

Not sure where the bear was, the women dashed outside and got in their vehicles to call their boss and the police. Just then supervisor Harold Wright drove into the back parking lot.

"I said, 'There's a bear in the shop!'" Kear recalled.

The three of them cautiously entered the store, believing the bear had been frightened off. But they were wrong. While Kear was on the phone with police, Wright went through the doorway of the storeroom and came face-to-face with the bear.

"I was six feet from it," he told the paper. "I told [Kear and Robbins] it was a big bear and to get outside."

Kear threw the phone down and fled. After officers arrived, they propped open the back door and then, from the front of the shop, made loud noises, forcing the bear to leave out the back. The animal ambled through the parking lot and disappeared into the woods.

Shop co-owner Patti Edwards said they had to get rid of all the candy and other sweets that the bear had gnawed on or might have touched. That meant dumping more than $500 worth of sugary goodies. Although workers and police couldn't identify the guilty bear, they knew at least one thing about him. Said Edwards, "It's a bear with good taste."

THAT'S A LOT OF BULL

An unwelcome guest barged into a house without knocking or ringing the doorbell. That's because he was an ornery bull.

On a wintry morning in 2010, Sally Joyner, of Peoria, Illinois, was in the kitchen while her 16-year-old granddaughter, Samantha Thompson, was relaxing on the couch in the living room. Both were in the upper level of Joyner's bi-level home, which had a front entry, known as a foyer, on a landing between two floors, each accessed by a short flight of stairs.

"All of a sudden I heard this loud crash," Joyner told the Peoria *Journal Star*. "I jumped up and looked down the stairs, and there was a humongous bull in our foyer." The glass front door had been shattered. "I was screaming. I went down a couple of steps and then I thought, 'What am I doing?'"

When she phoned for help, she worried that everyone would think she was full of bull and wouldn't take her seriously. "I called 911 and said, 'Please don't think I'm crazy, but a bull just crashed through my front door,'" she recalled.

According to a report from the Peoria County Sheriff's Department, three bulls had escaped nearby. Two were rounded up, but the third was seen running in the subdivision where the Joyners lived.

Of all the houses in the area, the wayward bull chose the Joyners' and let himself in by plowing through the door. Fortunately, the bull didn't go up or down the foyer stairs. "A flowerpot and all the glass were going down my stairs," Joyner said. "He moved around in the foyer for a while and then finally left the same way he came in."

The bull was eventually captured. The owner of the three bulls refused to talk to reporters, but Joyner said her insurance company had worked out a settlement with him to pay for the $1,500 in damages caused by the beast.

"I'm glad he found his way out," Joyner said. "I don't know how a bull thinks. With me being as hysterical as I was, he probably wanted to get out of there."

HEALTH NUT

Everyone knows fruits and vegetables are good for you — even a bear cub.

A young black bear casually walked into an Alaska supermarket, jumped onto a produce display, and helped himself to some fresh food.

The cub startled shoppers after he entered through the automatic front doors at Tatsuda's IGA supermarket in Ketchikan, Alaska, in 2011. Too scared to approach him, employees and shoppers watched the small bear stroll down the aisles before springing onto the fruit and vegetable display.

Assistant store manager Joe Stollar misheard an announcement over the public address system asking for assistance in the produce section. He showed up with a small net, thinking he was needed to catch a bird. He was surprised to see the small cub pacing back and forth across the produce.

Co-owner Katherine Tatsuda told local radio station KRBD the cub seemed fascinated by his image in the mirrored glass behind the display. She said he became nervous when a small group of shoppers crowded around him and videoed him with their cell-phone cameras.

When police arrived, they tried to coax the little bear away from the display, but he wanted to stay. So a customer stepped up, grabbed him by the scruff of the neck, and, while the cub bleated in protest, carried him outside where he was released into the wild.

The cub, estimated to weigh about 20–30 pounds, was considered on the small side by locals, who thought he might have been orphaned because they didn't see a mother bear nearby.

For safety reasons, the store got rid of all the fruits and vegetables in the display. Hundreds of pounds worth were given to a livestock owner, KRBD reported. Store employees then spent hours sanitizing the display case before restocking it with fresh produce for customers — humans, not bears.

A year-old black bear sauntered into a grocery store and chilled out in a walk-in beer cooler.

The 125-pound animal surprised shoppers at the Marketplace Foods in Hayward, Wisconsin, in 2009, when he entered through the automatic doors and went straight to the back of the store. The bear had no apparent interest in anything or anyone other than the refrigerated room where customers could select cartons or cases of cold beer. He climbed twelve feet onto a shelf and sat there for an hour, seemingly "beery" content.

Employees herded everyone safely out of the store and alerted animal control. Wisconsin Department of Natural Resources officials tranquilized the bear and removed him. He was released into the wild the next day.

The young bear did not drink any beer, which was a good thing because, after all, he was underage.

THOUGHTFUL INTRUDER

A black bear entered a house and helped herself to some food before leaving. But at least she was thoughtful. She took out the garbage.

While Wendy Radimer, of Kinnelon, New Jersey, was gone for a few hours in 2011, a mama bear and her three cubs walked into her woodsy neighborhood. Leaving the cubs nearby, the mama bear climbed through an open window of Radimer's home and jumped onto the woman's bed. The bear then wandered through the house, foraging for food. Every piece of fruit in a bowl on the kitchen counter was devoured except for a tomato, which the bear evidently didn't like and spat out.

She left dirty paw prints and slobber everywhere and broke a lamp after knocking it over. But in her own strange way, she did try to make up for the inconvenience she caused. Seeing a full garbage can in the kitchen, she picked it up in her teeth and walked back through the house. Still clutching the garbage can in her jaws, she jumped onto the bed and out of the window.

A neighbor saw the bear take the can up a nearby hill where her three cubs had been waiting for her to return with the groceries. She spread out the garbage and the family dug in for a feast.

"I was very upset," Radimer told www.northjersey .com. "I have three cats, but fortunately they hid from her. They were fine." Other than the lamp, there was little damage in her home. Radimer added that she was thankful that the bear took the garbage outside to share with the cubs rather than invite the little ones into the house.

VANDALS

SEVERE CRITICS

Two moose took offense to a statue of one of their breed and destroyed it.

Lars Johan Tveten and his wife, Anne Marie, of Bamble, Norway, erected a statue of a moose in their garden because they admired the large beast. But in 2005, two "art critics" showed up and gave their opinion of the cement figure.

That night the couple heard noise in the garden of their farm. "We thought the clothesline had blown down," Anne Marie told the local newspaper *Telemarksavisa*. When the couple woke up the next morning, "two moose were staring at us just a meter-and-a-half from our bedroom window," she said. Then the visitors turned their backs on the Tvetens and walked off into the forest.

It wasn't that unusual for the Tvetens to see moose outside their window, because their farm was located in the heart of moose country.

When the couple went outside, they discovered that their late-night visitors had shown their displeasure over their beloved statue by vandalizing it. The moose statue was lying broken in several places on stone steps leading down to their cellar. Its head was broken off. The statue was damaged beyond repair.

"We were surprised," Lars told the newspaper. "The statue must have weighed around 200 kilos [more than 400 pounds]. We don't know why they ruined the statue. I guess they just didn't like it."

BULL IN A CHINA SHOP

The common expression "like a bull in a china shop" refers to a clumsy, careless, or awkward person. But the phrase also could apply to a real-life situation that happened in 2003 in Lancaster, Lancashire, England.

A bull earmarked for slaughter escaped from an auction mart, bolted through a hedge, leaped over a six-foot-high fence, scaled a steep embankment, galloped across a busy street, and ran straight into the open loading dock of the nearby GB Antiques Centre. The 1,000-pound Limousin-Angus cross bull then charged into the sprawling warehouse store, which was filled with 80 dealers' stalls displaying expensive nineteenth-century furniture, pictures, brass fixtures, mirrors, art objects, and, of course, china.

For more than two hours, the half-ton beast roamed through the aisles of the 40,000-square-foot antiques center, scattering customers and collectibles like bowling pins. Some people were forced to dive for cover.

Of the two dozen customers in the store, the bull injured only one person, Christine Knight, 56, when he banged into her and knocked her down. "I was sent flying, and at first I thought I had been mugged and looked for my handbag," Mrs. Knight told the *Lancaster Guardian*. "But my husband turned around and said, 'No, Christine, you haven't been mugged. You have been knocked flying by a bull.'" She was taken to the hospital, where she was treated for a shoulder injury and released.

"People come here perhaps expecting to see a porcelain bull; they don't expect to see the real thing," store owner Allan Blackburn told the newspaper.

The bull caused $35,000 to $45,000 in damages, smashing valuable antique china and furniture into pieces. "Hundreds of items have been destroyed at a cost running into the tens of thousands, including some quite expensive furniture," Blackburn said, adding that a stall displaying antique mirrors took the biggest hit. "We think he saw his reflection and charged the mirrors," he reported. "They just shattered everywhere."

He said it was "pure luck" that the bull turned to the right when he came through the loading dock doors and didn't head to the left where dozens of stalls displayed delicate antique porcelain and china. The damage would have been much greater.

Blackburn praised his staff for evacuating the building and finally cornering the bull by dragging two large pieces of furniture across a doorway to create a barricade. The animal remained trapped until police and the bull's owner arrived.

"It could have been much, much worse, and I hate to think what could have happened," Blackburn told the *London Evening Standard*. "Now I really do know what a bull can do in a china shop — and we are picking up the pieces."

ANIMAL ARSONISTS

Pets light up the lives of their owners. But sometimes they light up the *homes* of their owners.

Osiris the cat started a fire that nearly burned down a house — by sleeping on top of the toaster oven. The ten-year-old feline was the pet of Lois Lund, of Port Townsend, Washington. When a dog was introduced into the household, Osiris was constantly being chased from room to room. To stay out of reach, the cat began napping on top of the kitchen appliance. His new sleeping arrangements almost proved disastrous for the entire household.

One night in 2010, the cat fell asleep on the toaster oven. At some point he got up and, as he stepped onto the kitchen counter, he pressed down the lever to the appliance, turning it on. Osiris left the house through the cat door.

A few hours later, the toaster oven overheated, causing it to catch fire. Lund told the *Peninsula Daily News* that she heard a popping sound in the kitchen and found the room in flames. She used a garden hose on the blaze after calling the fire department. By the time firefighters arrived, the kitchen and ceiling had sustained $20,000 in damage. The rest of the house was saved and no one was injured, including the cat and the dog.

Fire investigator Kurt Steinbach told the newspaper that the lever on the burned-out toaster oven, where the blaze originated, was still in the on position. All the evidence pointed to the cat, who had fled the scene of the arson and didn't return until the next day.

Lund said that since the fire, Osiris, who was named after an Egyptian god of the dead, decided it was safer to spend more time outside than inside.

A Jack Russell terrier mix named Storm dragged a lightweight, disposable barbecue grill from the backyard into the living room. There was just one problem: The charcoal was still smoldering — and it set the room on fire.

His owner, Jo Millett, of Bristol, England, had made dinner on the barbecue grill outside in 2009. She figured she would let the coals burn out. About three hours later, Millett was outside in her garden and unaware that Storm had other plans. Slowly and carefully, he dragged the grill through the open doorway and into the living room. He pulled it up onto the sofa, but the grill spilled the glowing embers. In a matter of minutes, the sofa caught fire, triggering a smoke alarm.

Firefighters arrived in time to save the house, a pet rat, and several pet reptiles that were in various tanks. The fire-starting dog was unharmed.

*　　*　　*

All Sparky the beagle wanted was a dog biscuit or two. Instead, he caused a fire that did significant damage to his owner's house.

According to WUSA News, here's what happened: Glenn Ross and his wife, of Franconia, Virginia, had left Sparky and his canine companion Brownie alone in the kitchen for the day in 2010. The couple had forgotten about the box of dog biscuits that they had left on top of the stove. Sparky hadn't forgotten about them. In fact, he was obsessed with snatching the treats.

He kept jumping against the front of the stove, but couldn't reach the box of goodies. During one of his futile attempts, his paws hit a knob that turned on a burner. It just so happened to be the burner underneath the box of biscuits. Before long, the box ignited, causing flames to spread throughout the kitchen.

A five-year-old neighbor boy was playing outside when he saw smoke coming from the house, so he told his grandparents who called 911.

Ross was about to sit down to dinner at the fire station when he heard a familiar address come over the radio dispatch — his own. Units from two other stations had been called to the scene and were already dealing with the fire when he arrived.

Firefighters had found Sparky and Brownie passed out under a table in the burning kitchen and carried them out to a neighbor's lawn. Paramedics put pet oxygen masks on the unconscious dogs and worked feverishly to revive them. The dogs were then rushed to the animal hospital, where they were treated for smoke inhalation and burns to their eyes. Fortunately, the dogs made a full recovery.

The kitchen was gutted, and the home had significant smoke and water damage.

From the evidence, investigators quickly figured out how the fire started. As for which dog did it, Ross was positive it was Sparky because the dog was always hungry.

A sparrow gave further proof why smoking is bad for people. The bird picked up a lit cigarette butt and took it back to its nest, igniting a fire that destroyed its little home. That was bad enough. Even worse, much worse, was that the burning nest was under the eaves of a store. You can guess what happened next. Yep, the store went up in flames.

By feathering its nest with a smoldering cigarette, the bird caused $350,000 in damages in 2009 to the

Crescent Stores in Leasingham, Lincolnshire, England, a village shop that sold groceries and other goods.

"It's a pity, really, because I like seeing birds around the place," storeowner Paul Sheriff told the *Daily Mail*. "But to think one of these pesky sparrows took a cigarette end onto the roof and caused all this damage is amazing."

Sheriff, who had owned the business for eight years, said he escaped thanks to a customer who alerted him to the fire. "I was serving in the shop when he ran in and told me I had to get out because the shop was on fire," he said. "The roof had disappeared and the upstairs flat had gone. I'd only just decorated the [apartment]. The shop was a total mess. All the suspended ceilings came down, all the electrics were down, all the fridges were broken. It was horrendous."

An initial probe found no evidence that the fire was caused by a gas leak or an electrical fault. But then an investigator for the insurance company AXA discovered 35 cigarette butts in several sparrows' nests in the remains of the roof. The butts came from customers who had tossed them on the sidewalk or street before heading into the store. The investigator concluded that one of the birds had picked up a lit cigarette butt and dropped it among the dry twigs of its nest, torching it and causing the major blaze.

"It's the first case of its kind that we've ever had to deal with," a spokesperson for AXA told the newspaper. "It's strange to think how such a little bird armed with such a small object could cause such chaos."

Lily the Chihuahua nearly burned the house down by playing with a cell phone.

The pint-size pup was looking for a bone to chew on. Not finding one, she chose as a substitute the cell phone owned by nine-year-old Aysha Sayed, who was sleeping in her bedroom in South Shields, Tyneside, England, one evening in 2011. While gnawing on the handset upstairs, Lily dislodged the battery. Her saliva caused a chemical reaction with the lithium in the phone's exposed battery. The heat from the reaction then scorched the carpet, which burst into flames.

The smoke alarm sounded, alerting Aysha's mother, Lynn Sayed, who was watching TV downstairs. Lynn rushed upstairs and grabbed her daughter and Lily and fled the house. Then she called firefighters, who were able to save the residence.

A search of the damaged house revealed the badly

dented battery dimpled with teeth marks in the upstairs room where the fire started.

"At first I heard barking, then the alarm sounded," Mrs. Sayed told the *Shields Gazette*. "When I came out of the sitting room, I just saw the landing filled with smoke. Aysha had woken up and was in a bit of daze, so I got her out and called the fire brigade. If we never had a smoke alarm, who knows what might have happened."

She refused to blame Lily. "It has left us all shocked. Who would have thought a mobile phone battery would catch fire?"

NUTTY GRINCHES

Squirrels acting like Grinches tried to darken a town's Christmas tree-lighting ceremony. But all they succeeded in doing was delaying the festivities for a week.

After the 2009 holidays, the city leaders of Braintree, Massachusetts, decided not to take down the Christmas lights on eight trees on the town hall mall as a money-saving measure. But the plan hadn't counted on squirrely sabotage.

A week before the 2010 tree-lighting ceremony was scheduled, the lights were tested. Many of them didn't work. To town officials' dismay, they discovered squirrels had chewed through wires on lights strung on four of the trees.

"We found ourselves in a bit of a nutty situation, but we're working through it," Braintree Mayor Joseph Sullivan told WHDH News at the time. "We will have Christmas lights on the town hall mall, despite the squirrels' desire to thwart Christmas lights in Braintree."

The mayor said he had watched the squirrels crawling around the trees all summer long, but he had no idea they were dining on the town's holiday lights. "I just figured they were gathering nuts for the winter," he said. "I didn't know that they were biting through our Christmas lights."

Officials ordered thousands of dollars' worth of new lights, which arrived in time for workers to string them up on the trees for the Christmas celebration. Although the festivity was held a week later than originally scheduled, it went off without a hitch, thwarting the Yuletide buzz-killers.

Officials learned their lesson. After the holidays, the lights were removed and stored for the rest of the year. Vowed the mayor, "We're not going to let the squirrels ruin our Christmas."

*   *   *

For four years, gray squirrels coldheartedly dimmed Christmas in Fredericton, New Brunswick, Canada. Every holiday from 2006 through 2009, the furry fiends feasted on the town's outdoor LED Christmas lights, although they disliked one particular color.

"They come out and they go up and they perch themselves in the trees, and they gnaw away at the lights — but not the red ones," Bruce McCormack, general manager of a business improvement group, told the Canadian Broadcasting Corp. "The squirrels, I think, are getting the better of us."

In 2009, McCormack, whose group was in charge of the holiday lights, said he thought he could outfox the squirrels by using larger LED lights. But the squirrels found the new lights just as tasty as the smaller ones — other than the red ones.

Dave Morell, a marketing director for the University of New Brunswick, told the CBC that the same thing happened at the year-round LED display in his backyard. "The squirrels in the neighborhood seem to like every color LED light, except the red ones," he said.

McCormack and his group gave up using LED lights. Instead, for the 2010 holiday season, they lit up downtown with large spotlights.

A WHALE OF A TALE

A frolicking whale leaped out of the water and crash-landed on a sailing yacht, destroying the mast and other parts of the boat.

Ralph Mothes, 59, and his wife, Paloma Werner, 50, were enjoying a quiet sailing trip in their 33-foot-long vessel in calm seas off Cape Town, South Africa, during whale-watching season in 2010. Southern right whales were migrating from the waters around Antarctica to the tip of South Africa to breed and feed.

The couple spotted a 40-ton whale about 100 yards away, pounding its tail on the surface of the water to communicate with other whales. Mothes and Werner were hoping to get an up-close-and-personal look at the sea creature. Instead, the whale got too close and much too personal.

"Suddenly it was right up beside us," Werner told the *Telegraph*. "I assumed it would go underneath the boat but instead it sprang out of the sea."

The whale flipped high into the air and smashed into their mast, snapping it like a matchstick. The couple watched in shock as the beast thrashed around on their boat before slipping back into the water. "There were bits of skin and blubber left behind, and the mast was wrecked," said Werner. "It brought down the rigging, too."

Sailors on a nearby boat took several stunning images of the whale shooting out of the water, practically on top of the yacht. Later photos show the destruction it caused.

"I just saw this huge thing come out of the water, and the mast crashed," Mothes told CBS News. "I ducked. I think Paloma ducked. The mast missed me by a few inches."

Werner told the newspaper, "It really was quite incredible, but very scary. The whale was about the same size as the boat. We were very lucky to get through it, as the sheer weight of the thing was huge. Thank goodness the hull was made of steel and not fiberglass, or we could have been ruined."

Although the boat was seriously damaged, it still floated. After checking to make sure the vessel wasn't taking on any water, the shaken couple cranked up the engines and headed for the nearest harbor. The whale, meanwhile, continued to frolic in the open sea.

CHOWHOUNDS

CHECKED OUT

Jack the Scottish terrier caused a lot of indigestion for himself and his owner when he ate two checks totaling $49,000.

Like many puppies, Jack loved to gnaw on things, and it didn't matter if they were edible or not. His human family was finding chewed-up cables, wires, and paper all over the house. "He ate all the paper that he could get his teeth on," said his owner, Roberta Kemnitz, of Santa Clara, California.

After receiving two checks from Bank of America in 2011 as part of an inheritance, Kemnitz left them on the table with the rest of the mail. But before she had a chance to deposit them in the bank, they mysteriously vanished. She and her son, Dan, searched the house but failed to find the checks. The pair did, however, find little bits and pieces of paper scattered all over the floor.

Their mischievous canine became the prime suspect. "We're not sure if he completely ate them, but I did find scraps of Bank of America material all over," Dan later told KGO News. "Unfortunately, we have a very young puppy that decided to taste them."

Added Kemnitz, "I was mad at him, but what can you do? He's a baby boy."

After Jack's expensive snack, the bank issued new checks. Instead of having them mailed, Kemnitz picked them up in person and deposited them in her account. She explained, "I didn't want Jack to have a chance to eat them again."

PASSPORT TO TROUBLE

Moses the basset hound ruined the honeymoon of his newlywed owners by gnawing on the groom's passport.

In 2010, Eric Mann and Brooke Blew, of Lancaster, Massachusetts, got married and were looking forward to going on a seven-day honeymoon in the sunny seaside resort of Cancún, Mexico. The couple had scrimped and saved for months for this vacation.

A few days before their flight to Mexico, Eric hunted throughout the house for his passport. He eventually found it on the floor with a chewed-up cover and teeth marks on several pages. Judging from its condition, Eric realized that his two-year-old basset hound had found the passport somewhat tasty.

Moses had a history of chomping on things he shouldn't. "If it's on the floor, it belongs to Moses," Brooke told WFXT News. "If it was anyone's fault, it was ours for leaving the passport within his reach."

Eric was worried that he might have a problem with immigration authorities, so he went to the passport office. "They said it was fine, and the bar codes and picture were all intact," he recalled.

The couple made it through security at Logan Airport in Boston without any difficulty. Said Eric, "They asked what happened to my passport and I told them, 'The dog ate my passport.' They laughed and said, 'Carry on.'"

The reaction was quite different when the couple arrived in Cancún. Immigration authorities at the airport told Eric his passport was unacceptable and refused to let him enter Mexico. "I handed over my passport, and that was it," he said. "We weren't in the office a minute and they said, 'You have to leave the country.'"

The couple was told they would have to return to Boston immediately. "It was awful standing there in the line," said Brooke. "I was sobbing."

Instead of enjoying a romantic honeymoon on the beach for a whole week, they spent only 25 minutes in a Mexican airport. The newlyweds were put back on the very same JetBlue plane that had brought them to Cancún. "The JetBlue people were wonderful," Brooke said. "They gave us drinks and food, and they upgraded us."

At first, TNT Vacations, the travel agency that booked the trip, refused to refund the $1,500 the couple had paid for the hotel. But after seeing news reports of how Moses had ruined their honeymoon, the agency offered the newlyweds a free seven-night vacation at a Mexican resort.

Brooke didn't blame Moses for their troubles. "This wasn't the first time he's eaten something valuable, and it won't be the last," she said, adding that he is "possibly the cutest canine ever."

PIGGING OUT

Ginger the hog had her name dragged in the mud after the sweet swine ate the main diamond from the ring that a grandmother had worn every day for 30 years.

Anne Moon, 60, and her husband, Les, 63, of Thirsk, North Yorkshire, England, were on an outing with their two young grandchildren at a corn maze near Yorkshire in 2009. The attraction also featured a petting zoo of farm animals, including kunekune pigs, a small domestic breed from New Zealand.

One of the pigs was Ginger, who always liked being petted. When she saw Mrs. Moon by the pigpen fence, Ginger ambled over to her. The pig was dazzled by the glitzy ring and just had to have it — or at least the big diamond.

"I've never been in such close contact with a pig before, so I put my hand out to let [Ginger] have a sniff," Mrs. Moon told the *Daily Express*. "It just clamped its teeth around the ring and wouldn't let go. When I did pull my hand free, the ring was covered in dirt. I gave it a wipe, and the diamond was gone."

Paul Caygill, the farmer who owned Ginger, told the newspaper, "The woman came up to me and said, 'You won't believe this, but one of your pigs has swallowed a diamond from my ring.' She showed me the ring, and it had diamonds round the edge but the big one in the middle was missing. She was a bit upset." He added that his pigs don't bite, and he was surprised Ginger had grabbed the ring.

Added Mrs. Moon, "Quite a crowd gathered around. One woman said she would be a witness if the insurance company thought I was talking porkies [British slang for telling lies]. But the ring has a lot of sentimental value to me."

The ring, worth about $2,500, had been given to Mrs. Moon by her husband about 30 years earlier. She said she had never missed a day without wearing it. The gobbled-up diamond alone was worth about $1,650.

The pigpen was immediately searched in the hope that ten-week-old Ginger had spat out the diamond, but nothing was found. Caygill was then left with the unenviable task of checking Ginger's poop for the valuable diamond. The gem was never found.

"I don't hold out much hope of getting it back," said Mrs. Moon at the time. "It's not so much a needle in a haystack as a diamond in pig poo."

EXPENSIVE TASTES

Coraline the basset hound had a thing about bling, especially her owner's $4,500 wedding ring. Because the ten-month-old pup couldn't actually wear the jewelry, she did the next best thing. She ate it.

The dog lived with Scott and Rachelle Atkinson, of Albuquerque, New Mexico, and often slept with the couple in their bedroom. Rachelle always left her wedding ring on the bedside stand at night. But one morning in 2011, when she went to wear it, the ring was missing. She and Scott couldn't find it anywhere.

That's when their suspicions turned to their basset hound. "She was the only one in our room, so we immediately looked at her — and she looked guilty," Rachelle told KOB News.

Assuming that Coraline would pass the ring through her digestive system, Scott had the smelly duty of searching through her duty for the next ten days. Every day he kept thinking this would be the day, but it never was. "I had to go through all the poos every day and squish them up and make sure there were no hard lumps in there, so, yeah, that wasn't much fun," he told the TV station.

The couple then took Coraline to the animal clinic, where X-rays showed the ring was unable to come out on its own because it had become lodged in her stomach. "There it was lying in the bottom of her stomach, and it was just too heavy to pass," Scott recalled. That meant the dog had to undergo a medical procedure.

To fish out the ring, the veterinarian first put Coraline under an anesthetic. Then the vet fed an instrument down the dog's throat and into her stomach. It took more than two hours before the vet snagged the ring and pulled it out.

Coraline made a quick recovery and was soon back to her old self of finding ways to get into trouble. Rachelle, meanwhile, learned that she couldn't trust her dog and has since hid the ring at night to avoid any canine temptation.

Luciano the Rottweiler also was attracted to precious jewelry. He gulped down a bride-to-be's engagement ring three weeks before her wedding.

In 2005, the former Deirdre "Deedee" Murphy, of Bethesda, Maryland, had taken off the ring and put it on her nightstand. "I woke up the next morning and saw my beautiful ring, and then I stumbled down the stairs for some coffee," she told ABC's *20/20*. "When I returned, the ring was gone. I threw myself on the floor. I looked under the table, under the bed, in the corner, behind the pillows, between the sheets, everywhere."

The mystery was solved when Luciano entered the room and all but proved his guilt by going up to the nightstand and, in front of Deirdre, swallowing the tube of lip balm that was sitting on top, right next to where the ring was last seen.

"I called the vet and said, 'I think my dog ate my engagement ring, and I'm getting married in three weeks.' The vet said, 'Well, we're pretty sure it will come out in about three days. Keep feeding him.'"

Figuring what goes in must come out, her fiancé Chris Lofft gave the 110-pound dog all the food he could stomach, hoping that would help speed the ring's journey through the animal. The couple sifted through stools with rubber gloves for two and a half days with nothing to show for it.

"After waiting sixty hours, Deirdre was freaking out," said Chris. So the couple took the dog to the animal clinic for an X-ray. It showed the ring was in the perfect position to leave the dog's digestive tract, so the couple walked him around the block until he pooped. "When he went, you could see the ring," said Chris.

Added Deirdre, "The ring was yellow gold so it had lost some of its shine. We took it to get professionally cleaned."

At the rehearsal dinner the night before the wedding, the couple put the X-ray in a silver frame with a sign that read, "Luciano — honorary ring bearer."

MONEY HUNGRY

Tuity the dog tore through her owners' cash — literally — to the tune of $1,000. The four-year-old chow/Labrador mix couldn't resist the ten one-hundred-dollar bills that had been left on the counter, so she ate them.

Tuity lived with Joe and Christy Lawrenson, of St. Augustine, Florida. One morning in 2011, Christy had put the cash in an envelope that Joe had planned to take to the bank later that day. She placed the envelope on the kitchen counter and left Tuity home alone for a few hours.

When Joe came home during his lunch break to pick up the money, the envelope was gone. Things looked suspicious when he found shredded pieces of hundred-dollar bills on the floor. "I saw a hundred-dollar bill almost ripped in half on the floor," Joe told the

St. Augustine Record. "I found three or four pieces around the house. I originally thought somebody had broken in."

But when he saw Tuity sitting nearby with a guilty look on her face, he quickly figured out what had happened. "She ate the bills, the envelope . . . everything," Christy recalled.

Not wanting to wait for nature to take its course, Joe fed the dog peroxide to induce vomiting. Tuity soon threw up munched pieces of the money. The Lawrensons then went through what came up and picked out the remains of the money. They pieced and taped the bills together with the help of Joe's mother and a friend who couldn't stop laughing, according to Christy.

Only one bill remained intact. The couple took that one and the other pieced-together bills to the bank, but received only $900 in fresh money in return. The bank refused to accept one of the bills because it was missing too many serial numbers. To get that one replaced, the Lawrensons sent it to the U.S. Treasury along with details and photos of the incident. Said Joe, "We just keep our money away from her now."

RING-A-DING-A-LING

It might have been hard to swallow, but Sam the golden retriever managed to gulp down a whole cell phone.

The six-month-old puppy was an eating machine, consuming not only food but things that were not meant for ending up in the stomach of any animal — things like dolls, pebbles, and clothing.

For several days in 2011, Sam was throwing up. His owner, Paula Connelly, of Stirling, Scotland, took him to the animal hospital and told the vet that she suspected the dog had eaten a doll belonging to her three-year-old son. The vet took an X-ray, but nothing suspicious showed up on the film.

Sam was sent home, but he continued to vomit, so Connelly brought him back to the clinic a few days later. At some point between the two visits, Connelly lost her cell phone. She couldn't understand where it had gone because she had last used it at home, but it was nowhere to be found.

However, her main concern was Sam's worsening condition. Helen Sutton, a spokesperson from Broadleys Veterinary Hospital in Stirling, told the BBC Scotland that the vet decided to perform an emergency operation on Sam.

The vet opened up the dog's abdomen to examine his stomach and intestine and discovered the doll. But there was a bigger surprise awaiting her. "She opened the stomach and put her hand in, and sure enough it was a cell phone," recalled Sutton. "It was like one of those old brick mobiles. It's amazing he managed to swallow it. He was only a six-month-old puppy. Without the surgery he would have died."

After the surgery, the vet called Connelly with plenty of good news: Sam would make a full recovery; a doll was retrieved — and, oh by the way, were you missing a cell phone?

Said Connelly, "I never thought the dog could have eaten it in a million years." She said the acid in Sam's stomach had made the phone useless. "I had to go to the phone company to say my dog ate my phone, but I don't think they believed me," she said. As for the doll, it had to be thrown away after being in Sam's stomach for almost a week.

Did Sam learn his lesson? Nope. A few weeks after the operation, Connelly had to bring him back to the animal clinic — because he had eaten a pair of pants. At least this time, the golden retriever returned them by throwing up.

OVERCOME BY UNDERWEAR

Taffy the springer spaniel had a wide range of likes when it came to food, or what he considered food. But his all-time favorite snack was, of all things, underwear.

By the time he was 18 months old, Taffy had snatched and consumed more than three dozen undies from his human family. Usually after a few days, his weird taste treat would come out of the other end. But his luck ended in 2007 when he ate his fortieth pair of underwear — a Bob the Builder undie. It became stuck in his stomach, requiring emergency surgery to remove it.

Ever since he joined the family of Eubie and Sharon Saayman, of Tamworth, Staffordshire, England, the dog had displayed a weird appetite. Prior to the surgery, he had gobbled an estimated 300 socks, 15 pairs of shoes, and a car remote. The Saaymans said they had spent more than $1,000 replacing clothing that Taffy had eaten.

"We always know when he's eaten something he's not supposed to, because he is quiet, doesn't run around as much, and doesn't eat his food," Saayman told the London newspaper *Metro*. "Nine times out of ten, nature takes its course and the underwear is then thrown out. But on this occasion [his fortieth pair of undies], he was in particular discomfort. Taffy hadn't touched his food for two days and lay in his bed looking sorry for himself."

Fortunately for the dog, Saayman was a veterinarian who quickly diagnosed the problem. He rushed his beloved pet to the animal hospital, where he performed a two-hour operation. That's when he found the Bob the Builder underpants, which belonged to his three-year-old son, Liam. It had become stuck in the dog's swollen stomach. Taffy came through the surgery just fine and made a full recovery.

Mrs. Saayman told the BBC that Taffy and Liam were best friends, so the dog was always following the toddler around while he was potty training. "Taffy would find the underpants that were left behind all the time. But apart from that, he's a lovely dog, and eating these things is his only fault."

Another dog from England, Deefer the bullmastiff, had slightly more discriminating tastes than Taffy — he liked eating women's panties, but not men's underwear.

His owner Lisa Hall, of Stapleford, Nottinghamshire, had wondered why so many pairs of her underwear and those of her teenage daughter were missing in 2005. The truth came out when Deefer passed the remains of a pair of panties while out for a walk with Lisa.

In the following year, he had swallowed at least 20 pairs of undies. But he began losing his appetite for them after one particularly frilly pair got stuck in his intestines and he had to undergo a $1,500 operation to have them removed.

When the veterinarian operated on the two-year-old pet, he found not just one pair of panties but two more taken from Lisa's dresser drawer and eaten. "We didn't actually notice them missing," Lisa told *Metro*. "It was only when the vet looked at a swelling in his intestines that we found where they were. It's the first time he has actually got a pair stuck."

While Deefer was recovering, Lisa and her 15-year-old daughter, Stacey, were under strict orders to put their used underwear straight into the washing machine.

Her husband Cliff said they had a clue Deefer liked eating strange things ever since the dog joined the family. "Even when he was a pup he loved to chew on unusual things," he told *Metro*. "Socks were his first love. After that he moved on to remote controls for TVs, and then he turned to ladies undies. I reckon he has gone through about twenty pairs in all. He nicks [steals] them from the bathroom and usually ends up passing them with no trouble."

Deefer, though, became picky about the undies he

ate. "My sons and I quite often leave ours lying around, but he's not interested in them," Cliff said. "He likes frillies and lingerie."

BINKY-LOVING BULLDOG

Lulu the English bulldog had a secret stash of more than a dozen baby pacifiers — in her stomach.

For her unusual appetite, Lulu was named the winner of the 2009 Hambone Award, presented by Veterinary Pet Insurance Co. (VPI) for the most unusual pet insurance claim of the year.

During a six-month period in 2008, David and Jennifer Zwart believed their daughter's missing pacifiers had simply been misplaced. Jennifer thought the "binkies" had been kicked under couches or dropped from a moving stroller. But Lulu knew where they were.

"One day I saw Lulu licking a dropped pacifier, and I scolded her for it," Jennifer, of Warson Woods, Missouri, told VPI. "I didn't pick it up right away, because I never thought she would eat it. But I turned around and the pacifier was gone.

"I took Lulu to the veterinarian and expected that an X-ray would reveal the pacifier. The X-ray was unclear, so the veterinarians decided to perform surgery. Midway through the surgery, they started a binky count, as they pulled out pacifier after pacifier. They had never seen anything like it. Over the course of six months, Lulu had swallowed fifteen pacifiers, a bottle cap, and piece of a basketball."

After the surgery, the contents of her stomach filled half of a one-gallon Ziploc bag. "The technicians asked if they could take pictures with their camera phones," Jennifer recalled. "We were all shocked, especially since Lulu never had any symptoms, and I had no idea all of those pacifiers had gone missing. Fortunately, Lulu handled the surgery very well."

Once the dog's owners became aware of Lulu's craving for pacifiers, the couple made sure the binkies were never left lying around.

POWER BREAKFAST

Rock the Labrador retriever loved the challenge of finding and eating foods that his owners had deliberately tried to keep out of his reach. His greatest accomplishment? He once ate nearly two dozen packages of instant breakfast powder at one time.

The dog was consuming the wrong things ever since, as a puppy, he devoured a chicken carcass that he had found in the trash. Another time he gobbled the contents of a bottle of vitamins. Then there was the day he had his stomach pumped after swallowing a pound of packaged whole-bean coffee along with homemade cashew brittle and peppermint bark.

So in 2010, it didn't come as a surprise to his owners, Don and Michelle Juen, of Maplewood, Minnesota, when the four-year-old dog once again got in trouble for eating something he shouldn't. "We had bought one of those bulk-size boxes of instant breakfast shake mix at the store," Michelle told Veterinary Pet Insurance. "We put it way back on the counter before we left the house that evening thinking, 'Oh, Rock can't get to it back there.'"

When they returned home, the couple discovered that Rock could indeed get back there and had broken into the large box and eaten much of its contents. "There was brown, sticky powder all over the floor," Michelle recalled. "It was a mess." As she was cleaning it up, she had an unsettling thought: "There are a lot of packages still missing."

The Juens took Rock to an emergency animal hospital, where he threw up 23 packages of the instant breakfast. "The veterinarian told us that it was the biggest pile of packaging he had seen come out of a dog in his life."

Rock suffered no long-term ill effects from the incident. Michelle said that within minutes of returning home, the retriever was "bouncing around like a mental case."

THUGS

TACKLING DUMMIES

Some animals act as though they want to play linebacker in the National Football League.

For example, a sprinting 300-pound bear broadsided a cyclist and left him sprawling on the pavement with a busted bike.

John Hearn was on his road bike in 2011 heading to work at Tyndall Air Force Base near Panama City, Florida, going about 20 miles an hour on U.S. 98. "I saw something big and black out of the corner of my eye," Hearn told the *Northwest Florida Daily News*. "Then it hit me, and I felt bear all over my leg."

The collision knocked him, his bike, and the bear

over. The animal was shaken, but got up and scurried off into the woods.

"As soon as I got hit, I knew it was a bear, so when I hit the ground, I was ready to run," Hearn said. "Then I looked, and the bear was already running away."

Hearn suffered road rash on his elbows, back, and hip, and pain in his neck. The frame of his bike was damaged and the back tire was ripped off. A driver gave him and his broken bike a ride to Tyndall.

"The bear hit at practically a ninety-degree angle so I barely saw him coming," Hearn said. "The bear packed a pretty good punch. It was like getting tackled by a furry, toned body in football."

A wild hartebeest antelope decked a mountain biker in 2011. Evan van der Spuy, 17, was pedaling through the South African bushlands of Kwazulu Natal during a bike race when the 300-pound antelope charged at him from the side at an estimated 30 miles per hour. Leaping into the air, the animal leveled the cyclist and then ran away without slowing down.

The "tackle" was captured on video by a racing teammate who had a camera on his bike and was trailing van der Spuy. It became an Internet hit on YouTube.

"The first time I watched it was at the hospital, after I received X-rays and I knew I was safe," van der Spuy told Matt Lauer on the *Today Show*. "I actually had a bit of a laugh myself just out of seeing how enormous the animal was. But it was scary."

Early in the competition, van der Spuy was several yards in front of racing partner Travis Walker when Walker yelled, "Watch the buck!"

The antelope's shoulder slammed into the cyclist and sent him flying into the bush. Walker yelled, "Whoa, holy cow! Dude, are you all right?" Lying in a heap, van der Spuy moaned and groaned before staggering to his feet and checking out his helmet, which was busted by the impact.

"From the moment that buck hit, I don't remember anything until the ambulance was on the way to the hospital," the cyclist told Lauer. Van der Spuy suffered a concussion and whiplash, but was soon racing competitively again — while always on the lookout for any more NFL–dreaming antelope.

A bounding deer should have been flagged for interference after it slammed into a cross-country runner during an important race, preventing her from qualifying for a state championship.

Sarah Glidden, a sophomore and number one runner for Hortonville (Wisconsin) High School was sprinting near the end of a 4,000-meter race in the 2010 Division 1 cross-country sectional in Wausau. With 100 meters to go, Sarah was closing fast. But so was an antlerless deer from the side.

Bolting from the woods, the deer collided with Sarah, hitting her in the shin. The runner was thrown off stride and partially spun around. Maintaining her balance, Sarah recovered from her shock and kept running. And so did the deer.

"I could see something out of the corner of my eye, and I thought it might have been a dog that somebody had on a leash," Sarah told the Appleton *Post-Crescent*. "Its hoofs kind of kicked me in the shin. I felt it pretty good when it hit me, but it didn't hurt real badly. I could feel its fur on my legs. It startled me more than anything."

Bruised and shaken, Sarah finished the race. Even though the deer didn't knock Sarah down, it did knock her out of a chance to compete in the state meet because she failed to qualify, placing eighteenth overall. Her time of 15:55 was 17 seconds slower than what she ran a few weeks earlier without any interference from a deer.

"I think the whole thing is kind of funny," Sarah told the newspaper. "It's weird, but it's funny." She added that although she had never picked up a rifle, she started receiving offers to join hunting parties for Wisconsin's upcoming gun deer season. Explained Sarah, "Hunters want me to go with them because they say I'm a magnet for deer."

CHATTANOOGA CHEW CHEW

With dogged determination, a pet bulldog attacked two police squad cars and ripped off the front bumper of one of them.

According to the Chattanooga (Tennessee) *Times Free Press*, Officer Clayton Holmes had stopped in the parking lot of a welding shop in 2010 to file a report when he felt his car shaking. Stepping outside to investigate, he spotted three dogs in front of his cruiser, including a bulldog that was chewing on his patrol car.

The dog latched onto the front bumper with its teeth and wouldn't let go, so Holmes jumped into his cruiser and slowly backed up. With the other dogs barking excitedly as if cheering on their canine pal, the bulldog refused to release its grip. Its jaws were so strong that it began tearing the plastic bumper. Holmes moved the car forward and back, trying to dislodge the bulldog, but the canine thug would not be denied. It had such a hold on the cruiser that it soon managed to rip the entire bumper off the car. As if that wasn't enough, the bulldog chewed two tires.

When a second squad car arrived, the dog attacked that one, too, along with two other cars driven by private citizens that had pulled into the lot. Throughout the whole time that the bulldog was turning cars into personal chew toys, its two buddies were barking encouragement.

Nothing would deter the dog, not even when police squirted it with pepper spray and shot it with a Taser. Finally, personnel from McKamey Animal Center arrived and captured all three dogs, who earlier had managed to get out of the fenced-in property. The owner of the animals faced a hefty fine.

The bulldog obviously misunderstood the slogan of animated police dog McGruff: "Take a bite out of crime."

A year later, an alligator chomped on the front end of a patrol car in Gainesville, Florida, and wouldn't let go.

Alachua County sheriff's deputy Victor Borrero responded to a call of a large alligator stalking the

Gainesville Golf and Country Club. When he saw the ten-foot-long gator, he pulled his cruiser to within a few feet of it.

While Borrero waited for the arrival of a trapper licensed by the Florida Fish and Wildlife Conservation Commission, the reptile took offense to having its space violated. It lunged for the deputy's Crown Victoria and seized the front bumper. With the animal's powerful jaws clamping down hard, Borrero put the squad car in reverse and slowly backed up. The gator dug in its feet and remained attached to the vehicle for several seconds before giving up.

Later, the trapper arrived and took the ill-mannered reptile away. But the thug definitely left its mark, causing significant front-end damage to the cruiser.

BATHROOM BREAK

A rodeo bull seemed so desperate for a bathroom break that he threw off his rider, hurdled over several high walls, and ran straight into a women's restroom where shocked women cowered in their stalls.

It happened at a rodeo in an indoor arena on the state fairgrounds in Minot, North Dakota, in 1985. After tossing his rider, the bull, nicknamed Wolf, chased a rodeo clown out of the ring. The bull then leaped over three five-and-a-half-foot-tall restraining walls and charged down a hallway before bursting into the bathroom.

"Someone screamed there was a bull loose," said Shaun Berning, a woman who was in a restroom stall when the beast rushed in. Cowboys who tried to get the animal out of the restroom told the women in the stalls to "stay down so he wouldn't see us," Berning told the Associated Press. "They said if he saw us, he might go after us."

Wolf had already injured one woman in the bathroom. Ironically, the victim, Barbara Deck, of Harvey, North Dakota, had been lingering in the restroom because she didn't want to watch the bull-riding competition out of concern she would see someone get hurt.

She never imagined that in the women's restroom a bull would injure someone — someone who happened to be her. When the animal charged into the bathroom, he pinned Deck against a wall, slightly injuring her left shoulder and arm.

Before cowboys could get him out five minutes later, the bull kicked a large marble sink from the wall, causing water to spray throughout the restroom. After the bull settled down, he left quietly. "They started calling him just like you would call a dog, and he just sort of went out," said Berning. Stock hands roped the bull and brought him back to his owner.

Tracy Pearce, Miss Rodeo North Dakota, told the AP, "What we had was a wild bull. That's part of a bull's behavior. They are unpredictable."

RUNNING WILD

Two lemurs escaped from an Austrian zoo and went on a five-day crime spree before they were captured in a hotel bar.

The cunning pair of two-year-old ring-tailed fugitives were residents at the Hellbrunn Zoo in Salzburg in 2010. When a keeper opened the door to their cage, they dashed past him and eluded capture for nearly a week.

While leading police and zookeepers on a wild chase through the city, the escapees staged a string of raids. They were spotted in backyards yanking down the wash from clotheslines, turning over garden furniture, stealing fruit from trees, and harassing domestic pets.

"We received many calls from residents all over the city reporting sightings of the pair," zoo director Sabine

Grebner told reporters. "But they were gone again every time we sent out keepers to catch them."

The lemurs' thirst was their undoing. They slipped through an open window of the Hotel Grünauerhof and stopped in its bar. "I couldn't believe it when I came in for work in the morning," said hotel manager Andreas Hasenohrl. "They were playing with the bottles, looking for something to drink. But I gave them a banana instead and quickly shut all the doors and windows."

The manager summoned zookeepers, who captured the fugitives and brought them back to the zoo. After their wild crime binge, the lemurs, who originally came from Madagascar, were named after the ruler of the lemurs and his long-suffering sidekick from the animated film *Madagascar* — King Julien and Maurice.

MOOSE ON THE LOOSE

A young bull moose didn't like being told to leave, so he charged a man, crashed through a fence, and splashed into his pool. Then the bully refused to leave. It took a rope and nine men — and more than four hours — to get him out.

About 9 P.M. one fall evening in 2011, George Trapotsis and his wife, Joyce, of Manchester, New

Hampshire, heard strange noises outside their home. It sounded like someone or something was walking closer and closer through the leaves and brush.

After Joyce turned on the light in the backyard pool area, Trapotsis went outside to the edge of the pool deck to investigate. He discovered the source of the noise. It was standing on the other side of a three-and-a-half–foot-tall wooden fence. "I was faced with this enormous, huge animal looking right at me," Trapotsis told the Manchester *Union Leader*.

No matter how spooked Trapotsis was, the moose was spooked more. Trapotsis suggested the animal leave. In response, the beast charged him, busting through the fence and running right onto the cover that stretched over the pool. With each step, the invader's hooves tore the cover until it ripped apart and he plunged under the water. He quickly got his head above the surface, but was tangled up in the fabric.

Trapotsis and his neighbor, Leo Desrochers, removed the torn pool cover and untangled the moose. "As soon as we removed the cover, the moose came up and it was just like a good day under the moon, just swimming around the deep end of the pool," he told WMUR News.

The stubborn 700-pound beast was in no mood to get out of the water. Fish and Game Conservation Officer Geoff Pushee and a police officer joined Trapotsis and Desrochers in trying to drag the moose out by yanking on a rope that they had tossed around his antlers. But that didn't work.

The cop called the nearby fire station and more help arrived. About a dozen men then engaged in a tug-of-war with the moose. They managed to move him to the pool steps in the shallow end, but then the moose refused to budge. After letting the animal rest for a minute, they pulled him up step-by-step until, at about 1:30 A.M., he came out of the pool. The moose had been in the water for four and a half hours.

"It was a long struggle and he was not a happy camper, that moose," Desrochers told the TV station.

Trapotsis estimated the moose did about $8,000 in damage to the pool, the pool cover, and the fence. But, he added, the photos taken during the ordeal are priceless.

UNPLEASANT PHEASANT

A pheasant with a serious anger-management problem harassed an older couple every time they stepped out of their house, forcing them to wear protective gear and carry a big stick.

For months in 2010, the ornery bird, nicknamed Yobbo — British slang for *thug* — would lie in wait at the front door of the country home of John and Carol Tucker, of Branscombe, Devon, England. Whenever they went outside, the pheasant would chase them and claw and peck at them, sometimes drawing blood. He often would run, hop, and fly after them while they were driving off in their car. Several times, Yobbo charged into their home when they opened the door. The couple had to resort to wearing gloves, hats, and thick clothing throughout the summer for protection.

"It's got to the point where I have to climb out of the back window as he's waiting at the front door," Tucker told the *Daily Mail* at the time. "It was quite funny to start with, but now it's extremely irritating. He hits my wife in the midriff, and I have to wear long johns when I go out because he tears me to bits."

Whenever Tucker, 72, and Carol, 64, wanted to relax in the garden or tend to their lawn, Tucker would lure the pheasant into a shed and keep him locked inside until the couple went back into the house or finished the yard work.

Tucker said he has had a love-hate relationship with Yobbo. "I like his pluck," he told the BBC. "I don't want to see him plucked. People have asked me why I don't just make him into a pheasant pie. I did nearly lose my cool with him the other day as he was being particularly aggressive. I picked him up and thought, 'I could just wring your neck.' But as he looked at me with his brown eyes, I knew I could never do it."

Ironically, Tucker is a retired ornithologist, an expert in bird behavior. Tucker blamed Yobbo's malice on his territorial instincts, adding, "He's either taking his frustrations out on me, or he's just a mad old bird."

A CAR WITH AN UNEXPECTED EXTRA

Like an eager car salesman, a big alligator was ready to pounce on the next customer who came onto the lot of an auto dealership.

The nearly nine-foot-long gator was underneath a Toyota SUV that Denise Anderson planned to test-drive at Sun Toyota in New Port Richey, Florida, in 2009. She was only a few feet away when the wily reptile made its move in the shadows, catching Anderson's attention. She did what most anyone else would do in a similar situation: She screamed and ran.

"I saw its eyes. Mouth. Its jaws. Its teeth," Anderson told the *Tampa Bay Times*.

Even though she was in flip-flops, she sprinted "like Speedy Gonzalez," said Michael Chaparro, the salesman who was walking over to assist her when he heard her scream. "She was freaking out, jumping, like a football high step." He couldn't understand what she was saying, so he walked to where she pointed, which was between two cars near the rear of the lot. By now, the gator had selected a Toyota Highlander to hide under.

Chaparro crouched down for a look . . . and gasped. "It was hissing," he recalled.

After deputies from the Pasco County Sheriff's Office arrived, the area was cordoned off and a licensed trapper was called. As a crowd gathered, the trapper — who was barefoot — lassoed the gator and got it into the back of his truck.

Anderson didn't want to get too close to the action. The only other live alligator she had ever seen was at Busch Gardens — "you know, a place where they aren't going to hurt me," she told the newspaper.

Although the dealership was on the corner of an extremely busy intersection, there was a nearby canal where the gator presumably came from. Chaparro documented the incident with his Blackberry and later put together a video that he posted on the dealer's website. Music that accompanied the video was Michael Jackson's "Beat It" — chosen, Chaparro said, because the alligator had to go.

AIR RAIDERS

Swooping seagulls launched regular air strikes against a bevy of innocent backyard pets that did nothing to deserve the attacks.

The mean birds tormented the four rabbits, three cats, and two tortoises owned by Barbara Smith, of Herne Bay, Kent, England, in 2011. According to the *Herne Bay Times*, the raids were like scenes from Alfred Hitchcock's classic horror film *The Birds*, in which thousands of vicious birds terrorize a town.

Although the seagulls weren't that bad, they did cause considerable trauma to Smith's beloved pets. "The gulls have been ferocious, dive-bombing my poor rabbits when they're out in the garden, marching up to them, and taking chunks right out of their fur," Smith told the newspaper. "They've even had a go at my cats."

Smith identified two specific gulls as the ringleaders. "I've seen these two gulls with fur in their beaks on a regular basis," she said. "One even came in my back door, ate some cat food, strutted down the hall like it owned the place, and was in the front room tapping on the window when I got home!"

Smith, a grandmother of seven, nicknamed the dive-bombing duo Gully and Ringo. She declared, "They're such a menace."

ABOUT THE AUTHOR

Allan Zullo is the author of more than 100 nonfiction books on subjects ranging from sports and the supernatural to history and animals.

He has written the bestselling Haunted Kids series, published by Scholastic, which is filled with chilling stories based on, or inspired by, documented cases from the files of ghost hunters. Allan also has introduced Scholastic readers to the Ten True Tales series, about people who have met the challenges of dangerous, sometimes life-threatening, situations. He is the author of such animal books as *Bad Pets: True Tales of Misbehaving Animals*; *Miracle Pets: True Tales of Courage and Survival*; *Christmas Miracle Pets*; *Incredible Dogs and Their Incredible Tales!*; and *Surviving Sharks and Other Dangerous Creatures*.

Allan, the grandfather of five and the father of two grown daughters, lives with his wife, Kathryn, on the side of a mountain near Asheville, North Carolina. To learn more about the author, visit his website at www.allanzullo.com.